Halloween at the Secondhand Bookworm

EMILY JANE BEVANS

DEDICATION

This novel is dedicated to my friend and bookshop
colleague, Tania Dumbleton

HALLOWEEN AT THE SECONDHAND BOOKWORM

CONTENTS

	Acknowledgments	i
1	SHELOB'S LAIR	1
2	IT	27
3	MISS JOLLY'S SCHOOL FOR PECULIAR CUSTOMERS	49
4	FRANKEN-HILL	61
5	PRIDE AND PREJUDICE AND WEREWOLVES	74
6	IN THE DUNGEONS	91
7	THE HOUSE OF COFFINS	106
8	APOCALYPTIC ZOMBIE WALK	118
9	THE HALLOWEEN BALL	133
10	THE RAVENS AND THE TELL-TALE HEART	163
11	THE WOMEN IN BLACK	181
12	FELIX JOLLY, THE RADICAL	194
13	GERTRUDE JEKYL AND MR HYDE	205

HALLOWEEN AT THE SECONDHAND BOOKWORM

ACKNOWLEDGMENTS

Thanks to my mum who helped me create some perfect
bookworm customers.

Special thanks to Anne Honiball

HALLOWEEN AT THE SECONDHAND BOOKWORM

1 SHELOB'S LAIR

Nora Jolly sat bolt upright at the sound of a
bloodcurdling scream. She had been happily sleeping in
her bed in the back room of her lovely sweet-smelling
flat above the 'Castletown Fudge Pantry', which
overlooked a little garden encircled by the walls of the
Duke of Cole's estate, at the top of the main street in an
ancient town in the south coast county of Cole, when the
ghastly sound had penetrated her dreams.

As her eyes came into focus she looked wildly
around for the cause of the terrifying scream. It
happened again, piercing and horrible and it came from
her bedside table. When she saw that her iPhone had lit
up, Nora fell back into her pillows with a groan,
remembering that her boyfriend Humphrey had changed
her text message alert the evening before, to a
Halloween themed sound.

"Very amusing, Humphrey." She grumbled aloud to
herself.

Her lips twitched slightly and she bit back a smile,
allowing that it was actually very funny and very apt.

For it was Monday morning in the last week of October and the first day of a week-long Halloween themed bookshop festival.

Nora worked in 'The Secondhand Bookworm', a rambling three story shop stuffed full of used and antiquarian books that were crammed onto every shelf and wedged into every nook and cranny in the endless rooms throughout the ancient Tudor building, like a labyrinth created especially to trap bibliophiles! It was one of two branches owned by Nora's friend, Georgina Pickering, the sister of Nora's boyfriend.

Georgina had decided upon the Halloween book festival the evening they had left an open air summer play several months ago. Nora had hoped she would forget about it because one of Georgina's ideas had been for her employees to wear Halloween costumes all week. Fortunately Nora's work colleague Roger's unremitting grim and glum protests had caused Georgina to enforce costume-wearing to one day, so Nora was free from looking like a prize idiot in her 'ghostly lady' get-up until Saturday.

The said costume hung on her wardrobe door, looking like an apparition. Nora stared at it, curled her lip and reached for her iPhone just as her alarm clock started, causing her to dive under her covers. Halloween always made Nora jittery. Waking up to blood curdling screams had sealed the theme of the week already and Nora knew she was probably going to scream at every Halloween themed prop, person and book.

Her hand emerged from under the quilt to grab her iPhone. She read the first message under her covers.

'Morning! I shall be arriving at the shop at nine to start putting up the decorations. Meet you there?' Nora read.

She grinned.

The message was from her sister-in-law, Cara, who was also her work colleague. In fact, Cara had met her husband Seymour Jolly through Nora only a year or so before. The two had married at the end of summer and were living in a flat between Castletown and Seatown, the latter town being the location of the second The Secondhand Bookworm!

Seymour was the owner of The Jolly Theatre, a popular and trendy Art Deco theatre in Little Cove, a village on the Cole coast where Nora had grown up. He was preparing for the opening of his play that week: 'The Woman in Black'. It had been giving Nora nightmares for months.

The second message was from Humphrey:

'Bet that scared you xxx'

Nora smiled and typed back.

'Will be there for nine xxx' She wrote to Cara. *'Yes it did! Xxx'* She wrote to Humphrey.

She then threw her legs out of the bed, got up and began to get ready for work.

It was officially Shriek-Week in Castletown and the council had gone all out to get in the gruesome spirit of things. Dark, blood red plaques had appeared on the walls up and down the streets, similar to the English Heritage blue plaques that featured throughout the country.

Castletown's blood red plaques announced horrific facts about events that had occurred in the town or horrible people who had lived in locations or committed crimes, such as the one fixed next to Nora's flat door. It read: *'Mother Death Cap poisoned her children here with death cap mushrooms in 1855'*. Nora hadn't been impressed.

After showering, dressing, buttoning up her The Secondhand Bookworm blouse, gobbling down some breakfast, feeding Beardie, her pet bearded dragon, his crickets, slinging her bag over her shoulder and stepping into her boots, Nora wrapped a scarf around her neck, ran down her stairs and stepped out onto the street.

"Boo!"

Nora almost shrieked as she nearly collided with Oliver Braithwaite, the owner of the fudge pantry located below her flat.

"Sorry, Nora." He apologised.

He was wearing a blood spattered top hat draped with cobwebs and carrying a box of fudge.

"That's okay." Nora sighed, removing her hand from where she had clutched her chest. "New delivery?"

"Sweet Pumpkin Pie, Black Liquorice Surprise and Blood Red Berry." He explained. "Would you like to sample one of each?"

"How can I resist?" Nora grinned.

She followed Oliver into his shop where his wife Gertie was already slicing up fudge.

"Morning, Nora!"

"Morning, Gertie."

"Ah, Oliver wants you to sample and review the festive fudge?" She deduced.

"I'm ever willing." Nora smiled, pondering a display of frog sweets.

Oliver opened the box, took out one of each and handed them to Nora with a grin.

"Mmm. They smell as delicious as ever." She said.

"Reviews back by lunchtime?" Oliver hoped.

"Ready for the Halloween multitudes." Nora assured, gave a wave and set off, sniffing the blocks of sweets.

She walked down the steep street, pausing to read several of the blood red plaques as she did so.

"*The plague was here in 1677.*" She read aloud and grimaced.

"The skeleton of a monk in his habit was discovered chained in the attic of this shop in 1905." She read next and arched an eyebrow.

"Three pickled heads were found under the floorboards of this house in 1724." She read and stared.

"Typhoid Mary once visited this shop." She read and covered her mouth and nose with the top of her blouse.

Shaking her head she passed a pile of enormous pumpkins outside a tea shop, a display of tombstones in an antique shop, a waxwork of a plague doctor holding an advert for the Halloween Waxwork Marquee by the main castle gates and was approached by a headless man handing out leaflets.

"Your mummy was wrong. There is something evil under your bed." She read aloud once she had accepted one. It was an advert for a play about possessed teddy bears. She shuddered and stuffed the leaflet into her bag, reaching The Secondhand Bookworm.

A gleaming new door greeted her. The door had replaced the rickety old one in a bid to stop puddle water shooting into the shop whenever the road flooded. It had passed a recent test of heavy rainfall and meant that Nora no longer had to put a flood board and pile of sandbags in front of it every day. The door was black and shiny with a sparkling window. A new step had been constructed too and presented a secure, pleasant first impression to the bookshop.

"Hello, door." Nora smiled and, as she was pulling out her keys, Cara arrived.

"Morning!" She said through her mouthful. "Are you talking to the door again?"

"No." Nora assured.

"Yes you are. I told you the wood spirits still inhabit it." Cara said and grinned.

Nora laughed.

"What are you eating?"

"A burger. Want some?"

Nora stared as Cara offered her a bite of her Big Mac.

"No thanks." She chuckled. "Look. I have fudge."

"Ooooh! Dessert for me." Cara smiled and they stepped into the shop as the alarm beeped and the two-tone chime sounded, the latter making Nora growl. The door chime annoyed her immensely.

The Secondhand Bookworm didn't open for trading until ten o'clock so Nora locked the door behind her as Cara ran to the alarm, punched in the code and then pointed in dismay at the ketchup from her burger-fingers now covering the numbers.

"First task of the day: cleaning." Nora said with a chuckle.

"Why isn't there a red plaque outside the shop yet?" Cara then asked.

"Oh. Paul is coming to fix it up today." Nora explained dubiously.

"Whu-hu-hu-haaaaa!" Cara said in her best impression of a ghost.

"I dread to think what it will say." Nora said, joining Cara behind the counter.

"Didn't you hear? They were all excited because they found information in the museum archives that there used to be a well there and a boy's skeleton was found down it." Cara explained, pointing to the flagstones by the door. "Before this was a shop all the past house owners used to hear the distant cries of a boy trapped down a well."

"Whaaaaaaaaat?!" Nora exclaimed. "You're joking?!"

"No." Cara promised, finishing her burger. "Ith the twrewth." She said with her mouth full.

Nora stared at the flagstone area located by the door to the Cole section before the carpet.

"That is hideous. People will freak out."

"It's Shriek-Week." Cara shrugged, still smiling and cleaned her hands on a wet wipe. She then turned and wiped the alarm pad clean of tomato sauce.

Nora shuddered and tried not to think of their red plaque.

"I'll go and grab the box of Halloween decorations then." Cara announced, tossing her wet wipe in the bin.

"Alright. I'll just turn the light on for upstairs in case we forget later." Nora decided.

They set off to complete their tasks.

At the top of the first floor staircase were five shelves packed full of travel guides, journals and diaries. The light switch was easily located behind a travel guide to Russia that had sat there for about five years. Nora decided to check the shop just in case there had been a disaster such as the roof caving in or a large flood. She headed into the front room that overlooked the square, walking on the creaking floorboards. After replacing some sheet music into boxes that Betty, her work colleague, had organised, Nora headed for the back room where the loo was located. On the landing before it were cases crammed with cookery books, humorous books and an overspill of annuals from the children's room.

Someone had left a dirty hanky on the floor so Nora kicked it under the bottom shelves of the cookery section with a grimace, hoping to remember to suck it up with the hoover nozzle next time she ran Henry around the shop.

The children's room was a tip. It always had a good rummage through at the weekend. The roadmap rug on the floor was covered in sweet wrappers and leaves and it looked like a small boy had left a sock. Tottering piles of Enid Blytons and Just Williams had been piled in corners. Nora ignored it all and headed up the stairs past shelving packed full of brand new Wordsworth edition paperbacks.

The top floor landing had cases full of crime novels in alphabetical order of author. The front room overlooking the square contained a myriad of literary subjects such as psychology, medicine, religion, sports, equestrian, crafts, occult, accounting and many more all arranged on shelving fitted around the entire room with more in the middle. The floor creaked and groaned as Nora wandered around.

"One day," she said to herself, "this whole shop is going to collapse!"

The last room was the attic room, located up a small flight of stairs. It was painted green and had several posters up including a map of Middle Earth. Thousands of paperbacks filled the shelves against the walls, only breaking for the window that looked down into the small yard below. The paperbacks were organised into sections with general fiction starting at the door and winding around in alphabetical order past the window and to a chimney breast on the east wall. The last few cases contained horror, sci-fi and fantasy.

Once she had checked there were no dead bodies or unforeseen literary catastrophes, Nora began back down the winding rickety staircase, noticing that it needed a good sweep and that the white handrail could do with a clean.

When she was back at the counter and had just turned on the computer, Cara returned with a very mouldy looking cardboard box. It was so large that she struggled in the walkway between rooms and squeezed through with an enormous grating sound.

"Whew. It's very mossy out there. I almost did the splits." She said, dumping the box onto the wooden stool behind the counter.

Nora stepped back.

"I hope you checked it for spiders."

"I did." Cara assured. "One ran away when I pulled it off the old loo. It's sealed so it's unlikely there are any in the box. While I was out there I noticed something very strange. A large object has appeared."

Nora stared at her.

"What do you mean?"

"It's on the estate agents wall just above the outside loo and it's belting out a heck of a lot of hot air, really loudly."

"Really? What on earth is it?"

"I'm not sure."

"I'll go and have a look." Nora decided and Cara followed her.

They opened the kitchen door, stepped into the tiny, freezing cold kitchen and opened the door into the yard which currently had a printed sign on it that read: 'Do not go into the yard until it has been cleared of slime.' Nora read it and laughed.

As soon as she opened the door the humongous sound of air being pumped into the yard startled her. A large white box had appeared on the wall. It was enormous and was making a huge noise.

"That's an air conditioning unit." Nora realised.

"Nice of them to ask us about putting it there." Cara said sarcastically.

"I doubt Georgina will be impressed. Obviously the Saturday staff didn't notice."

"No, they wouldn't have gone out because of the slime." Cara pointed.

Nora chuckled.

She shut the door on the racket.

"I guess after the immensely hot summer we just had, all the estate agent ladies were fed up with their make-up melting." Nora deduced.

Cara howled with laughter.

They returned to the front of the shop and the sound of knocking drew their attention. There were still forty five minutes until opening time so Nora pointed to the sign on the window. A very ugly man glared in, looked at the sign, rolled his eyes and stomped off loudly up the hill.

"Oooooh, look at all these pretend cobwebs!" Cara exclaimed, opening the box.

"Oh yes. Felicity bought those a few years ago. They fan out to make masses of the stuff." Nora said, making a note on the message pad to tell Georgina about the air conditioning when she telephoned. Felicity was a former employee of The Secondhand Bookworm. She had left to become a barmaid.

"We can cover the whole ceiling. Here's a box of small plastic spiders to place in it too." Cara said.

They unrolled some Halloween 'Fright Tape'. The yellow tape read '*ENTER IF YOU DARE*', the black tape had white lettering that read '*Haunted, Keep Out*', and the white tape had a dripping blood effect that read '*Zombie Zone!*' There were also battery powered pumpkin candles for the windows, piles of plastic human bones, an inflatable old crone, cardboard tombstones, plastic skulls, brooms and witche's hats.

They spent the next forty five minutes planning their decorations and started stretching out the cotton cobwebs. The instructions said, '*the more you stretch the more realistic the cobwebs look*' so they stretched like mad. Cara had stretched one pack over the whole ceiling and added a handful of small spiders by the time Nora unlocked the new front door ready for trading, to the sound of the two-tone door chime that Humphrey had fitted several months ago and was sadly still working.

A woman with a stuffed black crow on her hat was waiting.

"Are you open?" She asked.

Nora stared at the crow.

"Erm...almost. Can I help you?"

"We're looking for a copy of The Halloween Tree by Ray Bradbury." She said.

Nora looked around for her companion but the street was empty save for Hugh, the town street sweeper currently cleaning up dog's mess on the pavement while swearing and cursing to himself. Nora assumed the lady was including her stuffed crow in the conversation.

"If we did it would be in the attic room in the fantasy section." Nora explained, grabbing a box that contained free maps of Seatown and Castletown. "Or in the children's room on the next floor at the back. You're welcome to go and have a look."

"Thank you." The woman said.

Nora stepped aside for her to enter and she thwacked her crow on the door lintel as she stepped down.

"Russell!" She exclaimed and clutched at it protectively.

"Ooops, watch the door." Nora said.

The woman adjusted the hat, patted Russell Crow and headed off, pausing for more directions from Cara who was kneeling on the wooden stool pinning up the cobwebs to the ceiling.

Once Nora had put out the four black boxes filled with cheap paperbacks that stacked and clipped either side of the new door, she placed two postcard spinners onto the pavement, put on the brakes, added the sand pudding weights (small bags full of sand from old sandbags) and stepped back into the shop. As it wasn't cold that morning she left the door open.

"The lady with Russell Crow on her head asked for a copy of The Halloween Tree." Nora told Cara.

"Oh. Mr Carapace Clavicle Moundshroud." Cara said.

"Yes. It's like a Christmas Carol story but for Halloween. If we have a copy and the woman with the crow doesn't buy it I'll put it in our window display."

"Good idea." Cara agreed.

A man stepped down into the shop.

"I shat myself!" The man announced rudely.

Nora and Cara both turned and stared at him with wide eyes.

He was large and hairy and wore a blue boiler suit. His hair was immensely curly.

"Pardon?" Nora finally asked.

"I said I just shat myself. Can I use your loo?" He requested.

Nora cleared her throat and shook her head while telling him no.

"We can't allow customers to use our toilet." She replied, looking at him warily.

"That's selfish." He said.

"Sorry." Nora apologised, aware of Cara trying desperately not to laugh. "But we keep, erm, dangerous items in there. There are some public toilets by the short term car park and some new ones by the museum."

"I saw the new ones. They're mixed sex. I ain't a transgender." He said, turned around and headed off. "I'll use the ones by the car park if they're not shared. Then I need some new pants."

Cara couldn't contain herself any longer and bent over laughing, dropping her small box of drawing pins in the process so they scattered all over the carpet like tiny bullets.

"Oh, oh dear. There was so much wrong with that conversation. What dangerous items do we keep in the loo?" She asked Nora between snorts.

"I was thinking of the bleach." Nora smiled, beginning to pick up the pins.

"It sounded like we stored weapons or plutonium." Cara said, wiping her eyes.

"Well, Georgina said we can't let customers use the toilet because of health and safety. So I just think of people drinking our toilet cleaning products and suing us." Nora said.

Cara burst out laughing, stepping down off the stool to help pick up the pins just as another man arrived.

"Oh. Hello." He said, frowning at them rummaging around the floor.

"Hello, sir." Nora greeted politely, straightening up. "Can I help?"

"There's a book in your window." He said.

Nora glanced at the shelving.

"Yes." She agreed.

Cara snorted, still bent over collecting pins.

"May I have a look at it?"

"Which book is it?"

"It's blue."

"Okay. Do you know the title?" Nora asked patiently.

She grimaced as he walked over to the window and she watched him collect many drawing pins on the bottom of his shoes.

"No. But it's about Porsches."

"Oh yes, the car book." Nora nodded and flew at the window before he could reach for the book himself. "Allow me. There's a knack to retrieving books from the window display."

He stepped back and gave a small, condescending bow.

Nora removed two books facing into the room on the second shelf down from the top of the window shelving display case, reached in and took hold of a blue book. She turned it on its side to bring it towards her and passed it to him.

"May I have a look?" He asked.

"Of course." Nora nodded and went back to collecting the last of the pins.

The front room was already beginning to look like a spider's nest. Cara opened another packet of webbing.

"I won't take it." The man behind Nora said. "Not at that price."

"Oh." Nora opened it. "Yes, I recall it is more of a specialist book about the Porsche. For the serious collector."

"Hmm. But seventy pounds? I would pay forty."

"So would I." Nora said, feeling prickly.

"Well? Would you take forty?"

"I'm sorry, but I can't change the prices of the books."

"Your loss." The man said, turned around and stomped off.

The moody effect of his exit was spoilt by little tinny sounds on the flagstones because of the drawing pins he had collected on the bottom of his shoes. Nora's lips twitched.

"Time waster." Cara said, beginning to pull more webbing apart.

"Yes. There's even a price tacked to the front of the book so he knew how much it was." Nora said, replacing the book in the window.

"Some people like to haggle." Cara sighed.

"I need some fudge now." Nora decided and headed over to the counter just as the phone began to ring.

"I expect that's Georgina." Cara grinned.

Nora grabbed the receiver.

"Good morning, The Secondhand Bookworm." She greeted.

"Does Julie work there?" A woman's voice asked.

"Erm...no, sorry. There's no one by the name of Julie here."

"Oh dear. So where does she work then?" The woman asked.

Nora blinked.

"Erm…I don't know." She replied dumbly.

"You don't know? What kind of a shop are you?"

"We're a bookshop." Nora said warily.

"A bookshop? Oh, that's no good. Goodbye." The woman said and hung up.

"It wasn't Georgina." Nora said through gritted teeth.

Cara giggled.

The woman with the crow on her hat returned, shaking her head.

"No luck." She said sadly.

"Oh dear. Would you like me to see if I can order it new for you?" Nora offered.

"Oh no, that wouldn't be very helpful." Crow Lady refused.

Nora looked confused.

"Goodbye." The woman said and headed off, pausing to bend backwards really low as she passed through the doorway to protect her stuffed crow so that it looked like she was playing 'limbo'. Nora and Cara looked at one another.

A man appeared on the threshold. He wore a bright orange t-shirt with the face of a carved pumpkin on it.

"Can I just ask? Are the heads on the spikes by the castle gates real?"

Nora couldn't tell if he was serious or not.

"Erm…no, they're waxwork. They're part of the waxwork tent." Nora remembered.

"That's mental." The man said, turned around and left.

"I'm going to go *mental* before the week is up." Nora decided.

"Yes. Especially when the boy in the well starts shrieking beneath the flagstones." Cara said in a ghostly voice.

""Don't!" Nora exclaimed. "Now I'm too afraid to go and put the kettle on."

Cara laughed.

"Oh don't worry about the kitchen." She assured, stretching the webs out even more. "It's the ghoul in the yard you need to worry about."

"Very funny." Nora smirked. "Tea?"

"Wouldn't say no." Cara nodded, disappearing behind a mound of webbing as if she had been cocooned.

With a small smirk Nora decided to brave making a nice round of hot drinks, shrugging off the eerie feeling she had and ignoring the distant sound of echoing cries that she hoped were in her imagination!

"And as sumptuous as using a chocolate spoon to take a scoop of sweet pumpkin brains from Jack Skellington's head." Nora spoke aloud ten minutes later, marking a full stop with her pen and placing it down.

Cara's mouth was full of Pumpkin Fudge so Nora wasn't able to understand her laughing response.

"I don't know what you're saying but I'll take a guess that you're in agreement with my last review." Nora decided, smirking slightly.

She had made a round of tea and cut several squares of fudge from each of the blocks Olly had given her. Nora and Cara then spent their tea break devouring the sweets while Nora wrote her reviews on three rectangles of card.

October was usually quiet in Castletown but picked up in trade when visitors arrived mid-morning and afternoon. The Halloween festivities usually drew more people to the town than an ordinary dreary autumn day would. Nora wondered what they would make of the bookshop, which now looked like the lair of an enormous spider.

She gazed around the ceiling just as Paul from Castletown walked past the window heading for the doorway. He carried a blood red plaque under his arm and a hammer in his hand. He wore a black t-shirt that read: *I don't need a costume. People want to be me.*

"Hello! I have your plaque." He announced from the doorstep. "Cripes. It looks like Shelob's Lair in here."

Cara laughed.

"Thank you!" She appreciated, licking her fingers.

"That's not a compliment." He grimaced, though his eyes twinkled. "I'll just put the plaque up. Next to the window alright?"

"Go for it." Nora nodded, trying not to think of the well.

"Oooh, we must be in Cirith Ungol on the route leading into Mordor." Cara said. "That's where Shelob's Lair is located in 'The Two Towers'."

"Are you going all J. R. R. Tolkien on me again?" Nora chuckled.

"*Attercop, Attercop, Old Tomnoddy.*" Cara sang from 'The Hobbit'. "*Lazy Lob and Crazy Cob.*"

Nora groaned.

"You and your fantasy novels."

"Seymour's reading The Lord of the Rings. I can't believe he's never read it." Cara said, picking up a wet wipe to clean her fingers before she continued with the decorations.

"Hmm. We were all deprived of it when children in my family. Why, oh, why did you marry him?" Nora teased.

Cara grinned.

Paul began to hammer happily away on the wall so Nora gathered up her reviews to pop into the Fudge

Pantry at lunchtime and placed them with her bag under the stairs. Cara got back to work on the cobwebs, pausing to inflate the old crone.

Two elderly ladies arrived and gave them the first sale of the day: two postcards.

"Oooh, it's frightening in here." A lady with a very fake wig exclaimed.

"Don't look at it, Caroline." The second lady advised. She was carrying the head of a goose made out of wood.

"No, no I shan't, Velebeth. I shan't." Caroline agreed.

They rummaged in their handbags, found their coin purses and paid for the cards.

"Are all these books for sale or rent?" Velebeth asked.

Nora stared.

"Erm…they're all for sale." She assured.

"How quaint. My, my. What is the world coming to today?"

Nora smiled warily, placed each card in a small brown postcard bag and watched them leave.

"All done!" Paul called into the shop.

"Oh. Thanks. I think." Nora grimaced.

"Have a happy Halloween." He grinned and set off.

The phone began to ring again.

"It's about time we heard from Georgina." Nora said, watching Cara puff air into the inflatable old crone's arm. "Good morning, The Secondhand Bookworm."

"Morning, Nora!" Georgina's sing-song voice greeted.

"Hello!" Nora smiled.

"How's it going?"

"Oh. A bit slow. We just sold two postcards but that's it so far."

"Yuk. It's always slow in October. Hopefully the Halloween jollies will draw people to the town. Have you been to see the waxworks yet?"

"No, I haven't actually." Nora admitted.

"Take Humphrey with you. They're great." Georgina said.

"Why is the yard full of slime?" Nora asked, watching a man in a very tight beanie hat enter the shop to browse. The hat seemed so tight it was making his eyes bulge. Nora had the horrible feeling they might pop out.

"There was leak." Georgina replied. "One of the pipes from Mr Horror's antique shop next door was spewing out water for about three weeks. Because the yard is in the shade, all the moss has gone crazy."

"At least it's not poop." Nora decided, watching Mr Bulging-Eyes head towards the back rooms. "We've had quite enough of that for a lifetime."

"Quite!" Georgina agreed, also thinking of previous blocked sewage disasters that had taken place in the yard because of the Indian restaurant at the back pouring oil down their sinks. It had often resulting in large poops floating about the yard like boats. Fortunately Georgina had taken Max, the owner, to court about it in the summer and he had paid back in full all the Dynorod bills The Secondhand Bookworm had forked out to unblock everything.

"Are you going to ask Mr Horror to clean it?" Nora asked.

"Not a chance. The less contact I have with him the better. Apparently he was calling me names in the delicatessen on Saturday. Felix overhead him referring to me as a small, unfriendly, battle-axe."

Nora snorted with laughter.

"Sorry. That was rather unkind of him." Nora said, controlling her smirk. "Are you sure it's not romantic tensions between you?"

"Nora!" Georgina exclaimed, offended. "I'd be more romantically attracted to a slug."

Nora doubled over with laughter.

"Anyway. I've asked Humphrey to clear the slime next week. He said he wouldn't do it this week because he thinks it's very fitting for Halloween. I told him only earwigs and pigeons will appreciate it but he won't budge."

Nora giggled.

"I've decided to take you on calls this week." Georgina then announced.

"Oh goodie gum drops."

"No sarcasm!" Georgina warned. "We don't have many houses to visit but they sound interesting. We'll go on Thursday. The tickets arrived for 'The Woman in Black' at The Jolly Theatre on Friday so we'll all meet there at seven. I'm in London all day tomorrow looking at a large collection of books with Troy and Cambridge all day Wednesday so you and Cara are in charge. I told Roger that and he moaned about it for ten minutes. I'm considering firing him because he has been annoying me lately but Troy said it would be easier to make him redundant."

"Oh dear." Nora winced, feeling sorry for Roger.

"Yes, well. Something to think about in the New Year. How's the decorating going?"

"Great. Apparently it looks like Shelob's Lair in here."

"Oh! Are you going to rename the shop 'Torech Ungol'?" Georgina asked with a smirk in her voice.

"I take it that's what her lair was called."

"You really need to read The Lord of the Rings, Nora!"

"I'll add it to my New Year resolutions." Nora promised grimly. "By the way. A weird thing has occurred."

"Weird things always occur there! Fluffy. Don't lick Chubby. He doesn't like it." Georgina told her cat, warning him about one of her large dogs.

Nora giggled.

"What's happened then?" Georgina asked with a sigh.

"A very large, very noisy air conditioning unit has appeared in the yard."

"What?!" Georgina exclaimed.

"It seems to belong to the estate agents next door."

"And it's in our yard?"

"Yes. You can't really hear yourself think out there now. Not that there's much to think about out there. Except slime. And pigeon droppings."

"Oh that's not on!" Georgina scowled. "I won't have that. Can you imagine what it will be like in the summer when we have the doors open? Blowing all their hot air into your shop. I'll pay them a visit. When am I next in?"

"Oh." Nora rummaged for the roster folder which was kept under the counter. "Erm…oh, you're meeting someone here on Friday to look at some books for sale."

"Friday it is then!" Georgina said wrathfully. "I won't have people constructing things in our yard. Next Mr What's-his-face next door will be dumping his old tat in there!"

Nora supressed a chuckle.

"By the way. While I'm grumbling. Jason and Elizabeth have officially split up." Georgina then revealed.

Elizabeth was Georgina's niece. She had been dating her boyfriend Jason ever since high school and both had worked on weekends and during school or college holidays in the two branches of The Secondhand Bookworm until Elizabeth was accepted into Cambridge University. Jason was studying at Southampton University and had worked over the summer in the shops, but their long distance relationship had been strained.

"Oh, that's a shame." Nora pouted.

"Yes. Elizabeth is upset because it was Jason's idea. So I told her I wouldn't employ him here again unless she gets over it."

"Oh, I hope so." Nora mused. She enjoyed working with Jason.

"And Felix made a *big* mistake on Saturday." Georgina said, referring to Nora's cousin who worked weekends and holidays in the shops. "He undercharged someone for a First Edition and marked up two boxes of books all wrong. He said he was under pressure because of some haggish customers but I'm cross with him so I've asked Cara to watch him on Wednesday to see if he does anything else stupid. He's down to work in Seatown with her."

"Oh dear." Nora grimaced, feeling sorry for her cousin.

"Hmm. Right, that's all the news! Hopefully you'll have some good sales this week. There are some interesting things on about the town." Georgina said cheerfully. "Oh, hang on. Coming Troy. Alright darling, I'm almost done-did." She called to her American boyfriend and then sighed romantically. "Oh, he's being so helpful with mother's move into the annex. I don't know what I'd do without him."

"How lovely." Nora said politely.

Georgina laughed.

"Have a good day. Bye."

Nora bade goodbye and hung up just as a woman entered the shop and headed directly for the counter.

"Do you have a book about THE LICKING STONES?" She asked, shouting the topic loudly so that Nora flinched.

Cara stopped inflating the old crone in the corner and peered around the large black witch's hat that was almost full of air at the top. She was red in the face from blowing.

"Erm..." Nora glanced at Cara who shrugged.

A small squeaking sound began to emit from the old crone. Cara quickly went back to blowing.

"The licking stones? Is it a novel?" Nora asked.

"No. It's about Carlisle Castle which is said to be beleaguered by restless spirits as well as being the site of many gruesome events. A cramped and terrible secret room was discovered which had been used as a dungeon during the Jacobite Rising. It contains the 'licking stones' which are stones in the castle walls that were licked by desperate prisoners trying to obtain moisture."

"Oh my goodness." Nora grimaced.

"Yes. Truly terrible." The woman smiled enthusiastically.

"If we had anything I expect it would be in our topography section just there by the door. In the Cumbria section." Nora said, walking around the counter to look for her. "But I've never seen anything about the licking stones."

"Oh well you never know. This could be my lucky day!" The woman said optimistically.

The woman joined Nora and together they scanned the shelves. There was no sign of anything about Carlisle Castle, let alone 'the licking stones'. The lady seemed to become distracted by 'The Lake District Quiz Book' so Nora said that was a very nice book and perhaps the licking stones were mentioned in there but the lady just smiled and put it back.

"Well, sorry, we don't appear to have anything about it." Nora said, pulling out a book about Yorkshire from the Devon shelf and moving it down several shelves to the right section.

"Oh well. Never mind. Thanks for looking."

"No problem." Nora smiled, picking up some fluff from the floor.

As the lady left with a cheerful goodbye, Nora remembered the covered over well which would be located beneath her feet so she leapt onto the carpet with a silent scream.

More squeaks came from the old crone. Cara had stopped blowing and looked worn out.

"I thought I'd put her in the children's room with more cobwebs, at the end of the small corridor by the loo."

"Great idea." Nora agreed. "Shall I go and choose some horrible books for the window?"

Cara nodded.

"Yes. I could do with a break now to recover my wind."

"How lovely." Nora grinned and picked up the walkie-talkies. "I'll take one of these with me in case you need me to look for anything while I'm upstairs a-gathering books."

She turned on the contraptions and the sound of loud static filled the room. Nora went to fiddle with the channels to make sure they weren't on the same one as the taxis when an eerie moaning drifted out of them, accompanied by a clicking sound. Cara's eyes widened.

Nora grimaced, confused.

"You've tapped into the dead." Cara said in her ghostly voice. "Whu-huh-huh-huh. You're receiving their cries and their moans and…AAAAAAGH!"

An enormous bang caused Cara to leap up from the floor in fright. The inflatable old crone had popped and was now deflating like a very large sad, large witch-shaped balloon. Nora howled with laughter while Cara clutched her chest, breathing hard.

"Oh my goodness!" Cara exclaimed. "Horrible old witch!"

It took Nora at least five minutes to compose herself until she was finally able to dry the tears from her eyes and clip her now silent walkie-talkie to her belt. Cara ate some Black Liquorice Surprise fudge to calm her nerves and was smirking about the exploding old crone as she texted Seymour to tell him about it.

Suddenly, a familiar customer appeared on the doorstep. She noticed Nora before Nora could flee.

"Hello, Gina." Crossword Lady said.

"Hello." Nora replied, not bothering to correct her name.

For several months now Crossword Lady had insisted that Nora was actually the British actress Gina McKee and was working at the bookshop to research and prepare for a film role. Nothing Nora could say would deter the woman from her belief.

"Oh, what a pretty room." Crossword Lady said, looking at the cobwebs.

Cara paused in mid bite of some fudge.

Nora stared.

"Today's literary crossword question." Crossword Lady said, unfolding her paper and smiling steadily at Nora over Cara's head.

"Oh, I like puzzles." Cara said.

Crossword Lady ignored her.

"James 'Jim' *blank*. A character in Ray Bradbury's novel 'Something Wicked this way comes'." She said.

Cara was about to answer but Crossword Lady gave her the evil eye, so she popped her fudge hastily in her mouth.

"That would be 'Nightshade'." Nora answered.

"Nightshade?" Crossword Lady counted out her squares, looked up and smiled. "Wonderful. I'm so lucky to have you as my crossword partner."

"Thank you." Nora smiled politely.

Cara swallowed her fudge hard, on a laugh.

"Are you going to look around the Halloween fayre in the square on Slippery Saturday?" Crossword Lady then asked. "There will be many stalls. I shall be helping on the Slimy Critter stall. A gentleman from Walltown zoo will be bringing some tanks with the opportunity to hold geckos, cockroaches, snakes, tarantulas and others of God's creatures."

Cara gasped.

"Oh! I'm working in Seatown on Saturday." She said regretfully.

Crossword Lady ignored her.

"I'm working too that day but I might be able to have a look during my lunch break." Nora assured.

"Wonderful. Thank you for the answer. Goodbye, Gina." She smiled, turned around and headed off.

Cara looked at Nora.

"Slippery Saturday?" She repeated and grinned.

"Looking forward to it." Nora sighed, pinched a piece of fudge and set off into the depths of The Secondhand Bookworm to gather some books for the window with her haunted walkie-talkie.

2 IT

While Nora was busily putting a selection of
supernatural, occult and Halloween-themed books she
had collected in the window she noticed the Castletown
Tuk-Tuk whizz past. The Tuk-Tuk had arrived over
summer to give tours of the town and was driven by a
tall, fluffy haired man who managed to squeeze his long
spidery legs and tall haircut into the front of the vehicle
and chauffeur visitors about on tours or to destinations
up the hill for a fiver. It was usually painted black and
red but had now been painted completely black and was
covered in cobwebs. On the side it read: *Haunted Tuk-
Tuk Tours.*

Nora paused to watch it shoot up the hill where it
passed Marbles, a shop opposite The Secondhand
Bookworm which kept a gold mannequin standing
outside. Stan, the owner of Marbles, liked to display
various clothing on The Woman in Gold. She was
currently wearing a hideous Halloween mask and a
white lab coat spattered in blood. Two tourists stopped
and stared at it.

Cara walked past the window waving.

"Found some!" She said, stepping down into the shop and holding up a pack of batteries.

"That took ages." Nora said.

"I've been everywhere. Would you believe that I finally located some for sale in Jiao's room in Passageway Antiques. Foolish town."

"Really?"

"Yes. And I saw her Chihuahua in his birdcage again."

Nora chuckled.

Jiao ran a small room of interesting items and violent DVDs in a building owned by her boyfriend, Billy. She often carried her dog around in an antique birdcage and had recently taken to wearing 1980's neon fashion.

Nora watched Cara open the packet and begin to slot the batteries into the pumpkin candles for the front of the window. The ceiling was now draped with an enormous amount of cobwebs and the fright tape was on the door, the front of the desk and wound in and out the stair banisters all the way up to the attic. The old crone was in the bin.

A young woman wearing a white t-shirt that read '*333 – I'm only half evil*' strolled into the shop.

"Do you have any Breverton's books? He wrote Phantasmagoria, Nautical Curiosities, The Complete Herbal, 100 Great Welshmen?" She asked.

"Oh. I have seen them come in before but they wouldn't be put together." Nora replied. "Usually we display them on the end of bookcases because they have such nice covers."

"They do, don't they. I'm happy to have a browse."

"Yes, have a browse around the shop and check a couple of sections as well. The nautical curiosities book is put in our maritime section in the back room. I can't see 100 Great Welshmen in the section on Wales just there."

"Oh, the shop goes back and back." She noticed.

"Yes, and up and up." Nora smiled.

"That's great. I'll have a look." She headed off through the walkway.

Nora continued to place the Halloween-themed books in the window display. She examined a copy of 'Myths and Monsters' by an author called William Meikle. It had the illustration of a hooded skull on the front.

"*Bringing tales of adventure and heroics to the gas powered, three up two down campfires of modern life.*" Nora read aloud.

Cara grinned.

"*Adventure, terror and excitement all in one sitting. From vampires, to the wolfman, sirens, zombie monks, mermaids and many, many more.*" She read and shuddered. "I don't think I'll be reading that."

Cara placed the pumpkin candles in the window. The shop looked truly eerie. She then continued adding more small plastic spiders to the cobwebs that now covered the whole ceiling and much of the window.

"We'll win the Castletown Screamie Award at this rate." Nora decided.

"The *what*?" Cara laughed.

"The town council give it on October 31st to the best decorated shop." Nora explained. "Ugh. If you keep adding those spiders we'll definitely be the most ghastly shop in town. Eeeew, especially with that big one."

"What big one?" Cara asked.

"That big one there. Ugh, it's huge and horrible." Nora pointed.

Cara turned and held still.

Nora froze.

For a long moment they stared at a large black spider in the cobwebs above the Observer bookcase by the window.

"I didn't put that there." Cara said quietly.

"What?" Nora whispered flatly.

"I said, I didn't…"

Cara didn't finish her sentence because the enormous spider moved. It was large, fat and hairy and was wiggling its massive long, fat legs.

"Oh my goodness!" Cara squealed.

"Aaaaaagh!" Nora shrieked.

They both clutched hold of each other, watching the beast happily exploring the new cobwebbing. When they screamed again it held still, turned around and disappeared behind the bookcase.

"Shelob herself!" Cara gasped.

"No, that was more like IT!"

"IT?" Cara asked, her lips twitching with amusement.

"The mysterious, shapeshifting, eldritch demonic entity of evil that takes a foul spider form in Stephen King's novel. IT!" Nora shuddered, staring at the space where IT had been.

"I thought IT was a clown." Cara mused.

"That's one of IT's forms. Ugh! Now IT is in the bookshop."

"I think I'll win the Castletown Screamie Award after that!" Cara said, letting go of Nora.

"Where do you think IT has gone?" Nora worried.

"Back into IT's lair."

"Well I'm going to be paranoid now. And IT will be in IT's element with all these cobwebs. I'll have to wear something with a hood for the rest of the week."

Cara giggled.

"I think our screams scared it off." She decided.

While Nora was still shuddering, a man entered the shop.

"Oooh! Cool decorations." He said admiringly.

"Thanks." Cara grinned.

"Can we help?" Nora asked, bringing the collar of her shirt closer around her neck.

"Do you have a copy of Stephen King's IT?" He asked.

Nora and Cara stared. Then they looked at one another.

"We don't." Nora finally replied. "I had a look for it to put it in the window."

"We have the real thing though." Cara said.

The man arched an eyebrow.

"An enormous spider just emerged to terrify us." Nora explained.

"Ah, IT." He said with a small smirk.

"Would you like me to see if I can order a new copy for you?" Nora asked.

"No, don't worry. I'll have a look in the charity shop. Good luck with IT." He said and left.

"How weird." Cara said, referring to his timely request.

"Hmm. Spooky." Nora said.

As she stood contemplating how she would continue placing the rest of her Halloween books in the window with Aragog now in residence in the corner of the room, a zombie walked past. Nora stared.

"Er…Cara. There's a zombie outside." She said.

Cara ran to the window to have a look.

The zombie was walking out of step and making groaning noises. It had messy hair like it had just rolled out of a grave, a deathly pallor, brown stains around its mouth, various gross and bloody wounds, a blood spattered, grimy shirt and tattered jeans. Its arms were out straight in front of it like it was sleepwalking and it was carrying some leaflets. When it reached the doorway of The Secondhand Bookworm it stopped on the doorstep and stood groaning for a moment.

"Hi!" The zombie then said brightly.

"Er…hello." Nora replied, warily.

"Can I give you a leaflet?" The zombie asked. "I'm advertising two zombie walks that are going to take place on Thursday and Saturday this week in the town."

"Oh, how nice." Nora grimaced and took the leaflet from the zombie's decomposing hand.

"Everyone is welcome to join in. Just dress as a zombie and meet at the top of the hill at four o'clock. We're expecting lots of the living dead." The zombie said enthusiastically.

"That sounds fun." Cara grinned.

"It is! Hope to see you there." The zombie said and resumed its groaning, turned around and wandered off towards the estate agents next door.

"I think I need a lunch break." Nora decided grimly. "Mind if I go?"

"Of course not." Cara said sympathetically. "I'll put the rest of these books in the window."

"Thanks." Nora appreciated, heading for under the stairs to collect her bag. She paused to pick up her fudge reviews from under the counter. "Would you like anything?"

"If there's any soup in the deli I'll have a cup." Cara said, reading the back of a book called 'Real Haunted Hospitals and Mental Asylums'.

With a shudder Nora made a hasty exit.

After delivering her fudge reviews to a pleased and appreciative Olly at The Fudge Pantry, Nora walked back down the hill towards the delicatessen. The delicatessen was located across the road from The Secondhand Bookworm on the corner of a small row of shops that faced towards the top of the hill. It was one of three sides of shops around the little cobbled market square in the middle of Main Street.

As she headed towards it Nora noticed that a small sandwich bar had appeared on the cobbles so she went to investigate. It was called The Spooky Shed and offered many gruesome edibles, including an eyeball baguette (meatballs and tomato). Nora stared, grimaced and ran away.

The delicatessen was decorated for Halloween with modest adornments such as carved pumpkins, skeleton hands reaching out of the walls, balls of orange light and cobwebs.

Alice was behind the cheese counter serving a customer while Philip was stocking baskets of fresh bread in the window.

"Morning, Nora." Philip greeted.

"Morning. What soup do you have today?"

"Spiced pumpkin." Philip replied.

"Very festive. Can I have two cups please?"

"Certainly." He made his way behind the counter to the large urn. "Busy in the bookshop?"

"Not really." Nora admitted.

"It should pick up soon. I heard the Gorey-ent Express will be chugging into town this afternoon."

"The what?" Nora asked, looking up from examining a selection of quality pate.

"It's a trackless land train decorated like a ghost train. It will be bringing visitors into the town from the train station for the Halloween themed events and shops all week. Step on board if you dare." Philip grinned.

"That sounds fun." Nora smiled.

"Apparently they are all rickety carriages with eerie music playing all the way here." Alice joined in, wrapping a large block of cheese.

"I may have to take a ride." Nora chuckled.

Philip served up some steaming hot soup and Nora took the cups, said goodbye and headed back to the bookshop.

A delivery of new books had arrived and Cara had opened the box. Georgina had ordered five brand new copies of Susan Hill's 'The Woman in Black' so Cara was bravely arranging them in the window and on the counter. The rest of the books had been displayed and Cara was making price labels for them on the computer to print, laminate, cut out and tack to the front of the books.

"Ooooh, what soup is it?" Cara asked eagerly.

"Pumpkin." Nora replied. "More Bradshaw's Handbooks?"

"Oh, yes. As if we don't have enough already. Georgina still thinks they'll be popular." Cara nodded.

The books were brown hardback facsimile editions of a book used in great train journeys around Britain. It also showed a snapshot of Britain in the 1860s and was collected now by more than the average railway enthusiast, historian or anglophile since it had been featured as a television programme a year ago.

Nora liked to look at the original Victorian adverts inside that showed a variety of things including '*glass shades for the protection of all articles which may be injured by exposure*' and an '*important notice from Joseph Gillott, metallic pen maker to the Queen*'.

"These might sell well in the window." Nora said, placing the cups of soup on the counter. "There's a ghost train called the Gorey-ent Express heading into town this afternoon."

"Really?!" Cara grinned.

"I think it's named for Edward Gorey. Any sign of Aragog?" Nora asked, referring to the spider by the Observer books as the large Acromantula from the Harry Potter novels.

Cara giggled but shook her head.

"No, thank goodness. I think we should have Humphrey seal up the gaps above the bookcase so IT can't get out again."

"Oh that's a brilliant idea!" Nora agreed, pleased. "I'll text him."

She threw her bag under the stairs and was going to unravel her scarf but thought the better of it, wanting to protect her neck from Shelob.

As she sat down in the swivel chair behind the till to text her boyfriend, a regular customer arrived. Spencer Brown lived in Castletown and was known as the local 'Ghostbuster'. He was an avid collector of occult books and fancied himself as a medium.

He stood on the doorstep with his customary white hair glowing like a halo about his head, his hands in the pockets of his large black coat which was more like a vampire cape.

"Morning. Anything put by for me?" He asked, stepping down.

"Oh. I'll check." Nora said.

"Love the decorations." Spencer smiled, gliding to the counter.

Nora paused to watch him before continuing to look under the counter where the reserved books were kept.

"Thanks!" Cara smiled, arranging the plastic human bones around the base of the window display case.

"You have some great books in the window. But I already have them all." Spencer said, fiddling with the cobwebs above him.

Nora grimaced.

"Careful or you'll release Shelob." Cara warned as Spencer twanged a long bit of the cobweb above the counter.

"Shelob?" Spencer laughed.

"Hmm, yes, there's a very large spider behind this bookcase. It decided to come out and scare us earlier." Cara explained, glancing at Nora who was making an immense noise rustling the plastic bags that contained piles of books reserved for people.

"Let's not talk about that." Nora shuddered, emerging empty handed. "Nothing put by for you today."

"Ah, yes I probably have everything. Georgina said there could be some books that might interest me from a call she's going on later this week."

"Did she?" Nora asked, flatly.

"Yes. Some warlock wanting to cull his books or something. Hopefully he's an Aleister Crowley fan." Spencer said, examining a local guide book by David Bone displayed on the counter.

Nora screwed up her nose.

"Hopefully not!"

Spencer smiled slightly.

"Are you going to come magic potion foraging in the woods on Tuesday night?" He then asked.

"Pardon?"

"It's something my friend Mal has organised for Shriek-Week. He can find all manner of ingredients used in potions in the woods at the back of the Duke's park. We're hunting by candlelight and afterwards having a séance."

"Not likely!" Nora refused.

"You should do. " Spencer said with a twinkle in his bright blue eyes. "Especially since Mother Death Cap was a previous resident of your flat."

Nora pursed her lips.

"Will you be looking for fairies too?" Cara joined in.

"No. Goblins." Spencer said seriously. "There's defiantly a colony of fairy folk up there."

Nora wasn't sure if he was joking or not. It didn't seem like he was.

"Once I saw a will-o-the-wisp up there." Cara said.

Nora gave her a look that read *'don't encourage him'*.

"Really?" Spencer was interested. "Where was that? By the folly?"

"No, down by the lake."

"That may have been a water sprite." Spencer said.

"Oh." Cara arched an eyebrow.

"Or some fog." Nora suggested.

Cara hid her smile.

"You might jest, Miss Jolly but remember, if you hear anything go bump in the night in your flat you might want to make sure you have my business card on your bedside table. I'd be around in a jiffy to perform a spirit-cleansing" He said.

Nora grimaced.

Cara pulled a face.

"I'll be bringing Mal in here sometime this week." Spencer then said, checking his watch. "I'd best be off. I've got a letter arriving from David Icke. He's contributing to my article about alien reptilians among us in Castletown."

Nora and Cara stared.

"Bye." Spencer bade, heading off with his vampire cape flowing out behind him.

Nora sighed and shook her head.

"Next he'll be turning up in a turquoise shell suit to channel positive energy." She teased.

Cara laughed.

"Maybe he thinks the Duke of Cole is a lizard." She giggled.

"I doubt that." Nora said with a fond smile about the Duke.

Cara noticed and grinned.

Nora cleared her throat and took out her phone to text Humphrey. She wrote:

'Shelob is living in the bookshop. Can you come and seal her in please? Xxx'

A spindly lady with blond cropped hair arrived.

"Hello. Oh what a marvellous shop. Very scary." She said.

"Hello." Nora smiled, taking a sip of her pumpkin soup and almost burning her lips off. Her eyes were watering as the lady approached the counter.

"Do you have a book about The White Lady of Berry Pomeroy?"

"Erm? Is it a novel?"

"No. Berry Pomeroy is a very haunted castle in Devon. It appeared on the TV show *Most Haunted*." She said.

"Oh." Nora grimaced.

"It's very spooky. It has a real feeling of fear there, I felt it myself. And there are cold spots, and you feel a pressure on your temples and dogs hate being walked near it. There are apparitions of a black hound too and strange noises and lights." The woman said enthusiastically.

Nora wondered if she was related to Spencer.

"If you try to take a picture or film there, sometimes the film comes out black or all fuzzy." She continued.

Cara was listening with wide eyes.

"The White Lady was said to be a woman named Matilda who was imprisoned in a room at the base of a tower by her sister. She starved to death and now haunts the ruins! She will try to lure the living to death."

"That sounds lovely." Nora said faintly.

"Oh it's a very exciting place to visit. Although, I do feel as though I am being stalked by an invisible form since I got back." She said cheerfully.

Nora leaned back from her.

"Well, I've never seen anything specifically about Berry Pomeroy come in. Our section about Devon is in the topography section is by the door there, but I can't see anything about it there." She said, squinting across the room.

"Ah, well, I had to ask. I love the books in the window. Very spooky. Do you also have a section on needlepoint?"

Nora blinked, surprised by the diversity of the topics. "Yes. Top floor, front room."

"I'll go up and have a browse." The woman said and headed off, following Nora's arm gestures directing her through the walkway, and fingers pointing up the stairs.

The sound of a duck quacking alerted Nora to a text message received. She picked up her iPhone from under the counter.

'I'll be finished at four and can come to the shop and deal with Shelob. Dinner tonight?' Humphrey had written.

Nora smiled.

'Thanks. Yes, dinner would be nice. Also a visit to the waxwork tent? Georgina said we should go and have a look.' Nora typed, pressed send and looked up as Dracula entered The Secondhand Bookworm.

Nora blinked.

"Ha ha ha ha haaaaaaa!" Dracula said, opening his cape wide as he stopped on the flagstones by the door.

Cara almost dropped a copy of Bradshaw's Handbook she had just priced with pencil and was about to put on a window shelf facing into the shop.

"Ah. Prince Vlad the Impaler?" Nora asked politely.

Dracula smirked.

"I am here to invite you luscious brides to a Fright Festival on Friday night at the town hall." He said, brandishing a pile of blood red leaflets from inside his silk lined cape. "May I leave a pile of leaflets with you? It promises to be a ghooooolish event."

"Erm…well, you could put them on the edge of the counter there next to the till." Nora allowed, admiring his costume. He was a tall man with black hair slicked back, a whitened face, customary fangs and two trickles of blood sliding from the corners of his mouth.

"Thank you." He said and placed the pile where Nora indicated. "I like your lair. It reminds me of my own in the Carpathian Mountains."

Nora smiled.

"You don't happen to have a copy of Stephen King's The Shining do you?" He then asked. "It packs a sinister punch."

"No, sorry." Nora shook her head.

"Ah. Okay then. Hope to see you two brides at the Fright Festival. Farewell, farewell." He lifted his cloak to beneath his nose, held it so as to stare dramatically and then left with a flourish.

Nora and Cara looked at one another and laughed.

Humphrey had replied to Nora's text so she picked up her iPhone to read it.

'See you after four xxx' He said.

She smiled and then looked up at the sound of the heavy trundling of wheels approaching. Nora noticed the emergence of what was unmistakably The Gorey-ent Express. It was turning into the square from beside the butcher shop, large and impressive. Two rickety black carriages were being pulled behind a black motor unit which had been made to look like an old fashioned steam train. The train was covered in cobwebs with skulls along the side. Green smoke puffed out of the top.

"That is the most incredible thing I've seen!" Cara exclaimed.

They moved to the opened doorway to watch as it came to a stop on the cobbles and an eerie off tone train horn sounded. It was so loud that Nora covered her ears.

"That had to be about 140 decibels." Cara grinned.

"My ears are ringing." Nora grimaced.

People were stepping off the train, many in Halloween costumes, to attend the Fright Festival, restaurants or other events around Castletown. They seemed to be thrilled to have ridden the train.

Other proprietors were standing in their doorways looking at the train. A couple of people boarded. Ten minutes later, the loud train horn sounded again and it set off, passing The Secondhand Bookworm as it did so, heading towards the bridge and the distant railway station.

Nora peered into the carriages which were decorated with shredded black drapes, cobwebs and orange lights.

"I think I'll catch the train on Thursday." Cara decided. "Then I can ride the ghost train."

Nora laughed, thinking that it would be a very Halloweeny way to travel!

At half past four, Nora and Cara were sitting drinking hot tea and lamenting the lack of bookworm customers when Humphrey arrived.

"Where's Shelob then?" He asked, holding up a large tube of silicone sealant in a bright red gun.

"Ah, Frodo." Nora welcomed.

Humphrey laughed.

"Wow, this is definitely like a Halloween coven." He said, looking around. "No wonder you attracted an Ungoliant."

"Are you a Tolkien fan too?!" Cara grinned.

"Georgina read them to me when I was boy and then made me read them again as a teen." He said.

Nora pointed towards the bookcase to the right of the window.

"She came from there." She pointed with a shiver.

The bookcase was narrow and contained a whole collection of Observer books, small pocket sized books of various topics such as birds, fungi, big bands and number 99 which was The Observer Book of Observer Books. The bookcase had been fixed there when the building had first converted from a house into a shop several decades ago. In fact, according to a woman who used to live there and who had visited the shop last Christmas, it had once been a tobacconist which had supplied J. R. R Tolkien his tobacco. Nora thought Shelob's appearance was to remind her to read Lord of the Rings and put Georgina's mind at ease.

"Well, she was probably attracted by your forest of cobwebs." Humphrey said, approaching. "I'll seal the edges and she shouldn't be able to emerge. I'm sure she can make her way through the framework and out into the street."

"Oh I hope not." Nora grimaced.

They watched as Humphrey positioned his sealant gun along the top and squeezed out the silicone. The smell was strong and soon they all felt light headed. Nora began to relax knowing all gaps and openings had been closed.

"Thank you." Nora appreciated once Humphrey had finished.

"No problem." He said. "By the way, I see some stocks have been set up in the town square."

Nora and Cara scrambled around the counter and moved to the window to stare out into the street. In fact, as well as a low wooden stocks for securing legs, there was also a large wooden pillory made of wood and metal on a post for securing the head and hands now positioned on the cobbles.

"Do you think people will be put in them?" Cara wondered.

Humphrey joined them, peering out into the street.

"It's part of the Spooky Trail." He said, biting into a Mars Bar. "I was talking to Paul as he was fixing one of those red plaques you like onto a wall by the charity shop. Apparently a notorious highway man who removed people's tongues once took refuge in the

42

charity shop. I doubt it was a charity shop at the time of course."

Nora snorted.

"Well, I don't fancy going on this Spooky Trial." Nora decided.

"Oh I would." Cara said. "I'll ask Seymour to do it, too. He loves Halloween."

"Hmm, yes he does." Nora remembered grimly.

"There are some ghost shaped cakes in the deli. Would you like one?" Humphrey asked Nora and Cara.

"Oh yes please." They accepted in unison.

Humphrey headed off, leaving them to start tidying the shop and begin to bring things in from outside to close up.

"Are you closing?" A man asked, strolling into the shop. "I won't be long." He said, before they could answer, and scuttled off through the walkway and began climbing the stairs.

Cara shook her head.

"One to throw out at five o'clock no doubt." She sighed.

There were some end-of-day requests from the Seatown branch on Skype chat. Nora's colleague Roger was working with Agnes, the latter of whom was on a university break and working a few days that week. The message read:

'Please can you see if you have a copy of Jamie Oliver '5 Ingredients' in cookery section? Also, The Handmaid's Tale by Margaret Atwood in paperback fiction. Thank you, Roger.

Cara ran and had a look in the relevant sections while Nora sold a book about werewolves from the window, three postcards and a mug.

A few people were milling about browsing when Humphrey returned with the cakes. And Cara came back to tell Roger and Agnes she had no luck locating their requests.

"They're vanilla sponge with raspberry filling and the white is fondant icing." Humphrey told them, opening the paper bags.

They wiped their hands on wet wipes and stood munching the cakes happily.

"Oh look, I just ate the ghost's head." Cara said.

Nora laughed through her mouthful.

"Who knew you could eat ghosts." Humphrey shrugged, biting the folds of its cloak.

"Some can take material form." Cara said.

Nora smiled.

At closing time Humphrey helped bring the postcard spinners, black boxes of paperbacks and free map box from outside. He then used his own key to lock the door. Cara headed upstairs to usher the maundering customers out while Nora added up the day's takings.

"Oh dear. Barely over two hundred pounds today." She sighed, turning the till to cash up.

"Autumn's always quiet." Humphrey said, adjusting some cobwebs. "Are you going to leave the pumpkin lights on?"

"Yes, they can remain on for the week. They'll look good at night." Nora nodded.

The zombie walked past in the twilight. Nora stared a moment and then began to cash up.

"Thanks for letting me browse." The man who had marched in early said as he came into the front. "I just wanted to kill some time before my train."

Humphrey unlocked the door.

"Our pleasure, sir. Have a good evening." He bade, letting him out.

"Thank you! I'm sure I will." The man smiled and headed out into the street.

Cara locked up the kitchen, turned off all the lights, they grabbed their coats, bags, said '*byeeeeeee*' to the Seatown branch on Skype chat, turned off the computer, set the alarm, turned off the front lights and scrambled out so the alarm could set.

Humphrey locked up as Cara and Nora hugged.

"Have a good evening." Cara bade.

"You too." Nora waved and turned to Humphrey as he took hold of her hand.

"Nice day?" He asked after he had kissed her.

"Interesting." Nora admitted.

They started walking past the estate agents, heading for the waxwork tent by the main castle gates. On the way they stopped to look at the Halloween displays in the barber shop window as well as the charity shop window. There were some gothic objects in the antique shop just before the post office on the corner, such as a black parasol, a black leather plague doctor mask, gargoyle statues, iron candlesticks and a large section of stained glass window from a church.

The post office had a lot of steampunk items surrounded by cobwebs in their small arched windows which looked very effective. Nora and Humphrey examined binoculars, goggles, hats, a backpack time machine, vambrace and a lantern with endless small cogs surrounding them all. Humphrey liked the mix of Victorian, American Wild West and retro futuristic themes.

The Halloween Waxwork Marquee was a large black circus tent in the public garden next to the main castle gates. Real flame torches burned either side of two tall iron gates that had been fitted to the usual small wooden ones.

The public garden was surrounded by a low privet hedge that led right up to the tall stone castle walls. A small marquee ticket booth was just outside the gates manned by a ghostly pirate.

"Avast!" The pirate said as they came to the booth. "Welcome to ye olde Halloween Waxwork Marquee."

"Thanks." Humphrey smiled. "Two adults please."

"One landlubber and one wench." The pirate said, tearing two small blue tickets from a book and passing them to Humphrey. "Arrrr. That'll be five gold doubloons, me hearties. And no hornswaggling."

Nora grinned and he winked at her.

Humphrey passed a five pound note to the pirate. He took it and waved them through the gates.

"Heave ho!" He said, ushering them on.

They entered the garden and were greeted by an old witch who took their tickets, cackled loudly and practically pushed them through the doorway into the tent. Nora and Humphrey blinked.

It was dark inside with eerie organ music playing. The waxworks stood on individual wooden platforms. Cobwebs hung all around, the tent walls were spattered with blood. Every so often a small blast of dry ice pumped out. The lighting was low, orange and blue. Three other people were inside; a man and a woman and young girl with a long blond plait.

They made their way around the exhibits, looking at excellent and very eerie effigies of Jack the Ripper, a plague doctor, Typhoid Mary, Mrs Lovett holding her pies, Dracula, Sweeny Todd and more, each with information plaques about them to read. A sudden sound made Humphrey and Nora turn. A crouched figure was approaching them with a loud banging noise, really fast.

Nora screamed loudly in terror. The young girl happened to be standing beside her so Nora automatically clutched hold of her plait and pulled hard while screaming. Just as the figure reached them it stood up to reveal a laughing man. He had been wearing a heavy wax cloak and banging a stick against the wooden platforms.

"Ha ha ha, oh the looks on your faces! It works every time!" The man chortled. "I had to make you scream, it's part of the Halloween experience."

"I am so sorry." Nora apologised to the girl, letting go of her plait.

The girl's eyes were watering in pain but she grinned.

"That's okay! It made it more of a fright." She said, skipping off towards Mrs Lovett.

Humphrey was trying his best not to dissolve with laughter. Nora grimaced.

"I don't know why I grabbed the poor child's hair."

"It was a reaction." Humphrey said, wrapping his arm around Nora's shoulder and kissing her head. "You were so scared."

"Terrified more like it." Nora mumbled. "Let's get out of here."

Humphrey led the way and they left the tent as the man was getting ready to repeat his hunched over figure for the laughing couple with the girl. They passed the old crone who cackled at them and walked by the ticket marquee where the pirate called out:

"Thar she blows!"

Nora glanced back.

"Isn't that what a pirate says when he spots a whale from a ship?"

Humphrey snorted with laughter against Nora's hair.

"Come on Shamu." He teased.

"I'm a killer whale?!" Nora exclaimed. "You know that Humphrey the Whale was one of the most famous humpback whales in history? He swam into San Francisco Bay."

"What a pair of leviathans we are." Humphrey the Human chuckled. "Let's go eat!"

Nora chuckled and they began to walk away.

"The Duke's Pie?" Humphrey asked, referring to the famous restaurant near Nora's flat up the hill which was more like a smuggling tavern.

"As long as there are no pirates." Nora said, glanced back over her shoulder at The Halloween Waxwork Marquee and sighed.

3 MISS JOLLY'S SCHOOL FOR PECULIAR CUSTOMERS

Although Humphrey had sealed up the gaps in the bookcase where IT had disappeared, Nora arrived at The Secondhand Bookworm the following day wearing a zip up hoodie over her bookworm shirt. She also wore a small cotton scarf decorated with skulls, cringing at the thought of an enormous spider dropping down her neck.

Roger was opening up the shop.

"What the…?" He said when he saw the decorations. He shook his head, stepping inside. "Is this your handy work, Miss Jolly?"

"Mine and Cara's." Nora replied, closing and locking the door behind her.

"So I have to duck cobwebs all day. How nice." Roger moaned glumly.

"At least you're not in your Frankenstein get up." Nora pointed out.

Roger scowled.

He punched the code into the alarm and unbuttoned his coat while Nora threw her bag under the stairs. It was a windy day so the blind that hung over the window outside was rattling against the wall.

"What time would you like lunch today?" Roger asked.

"Lunch? I've only just had breakfast."

"I like to be organised." Roger said.

"Well, I suppose I could go at one."

"I'll go at one thirty then." Roger decided, hung up his coat and switched on the computer. "Would you like a cup of tea?"

"Okay, then. Thanks." Nora smiled.

"I'll go and put the kettle on."

Roger headed off.

"Can you turn the lights on for upstairs too?" Nora called.

"Okay, Sergeant Major!" Roger called back.

Nora rolled her eyes, filling up the till with the cash float.

Someone posted a leaflet through the letterbox. Nora walked around the counter and almost tripped on a stack of railway books Cara had dropped into the shop on her way over to the Seatown branch.

"Argh. Something for Roger to do today." Nora muttered, glanced towards Shelob's Lair, tightened her collar and hurried past it to the door.

The leaflet was bright orange. It was advertising Halloween craft activities taking place down Market Street that day, where children and the young at heart could make their own Halloween hat, spooky masks, monster sticks, bats and Halloween lanterns.

Nora thought about suggesting Roger should go along but decided he wouldn't find it funny. It was almost ten o'clock and a shadow loomed up to the window in the door. Nora unlocked and opened it to the accompaniment of the two-toned door chime.

The shadow belonged to a big, bald man.

"Nietzsche?" He asked.

"Oh. Yes probably a new copy in a Wordsworth edition."

"Nope." He refused, turned around and left.

Nora stared after him.

A woman shuffled up to the door.

"D'you buy books?"

"Yes, we do." Nora nodded.

"I have loads in the boot of my car. Can you take a look?" She asked, picking her nose.

Nora grimaced, wondering if her books were all covered in boogers.

"Yes, I can. Where are you parked?"

"Behind that blue van there." She said, pointing up the hill.

Far in the distance Nora spotted a blue van.

"Okay. I'll just ask my colleague to come into the front room and man the till." Nora leaned back into the room.

Roger had arrived with two steaming mugs of tea. He took a sip and burned his mouth so stood muttering and frowning angrily.

"Roger? I'm just going to look at someone's books in the boot of their car." Nora called in.

"Don't get kidnapped." He warned.

"I'll try not to." Nora assured and set off with the lady.

"I wasn't sure if you bought books. I came into town to see if I could sell some cremation urns at an antique shop. They contain the ashes of several relatives I never even met, so I have no use for them. I inherited them from a distant aunt." The woman said.

Nora almost tripped over.

"Oh. Did you manage to sell them?"

"I did, but I had a hard time of it. People looked at me as if I was mad! In the end a Chinese woman bought them from me down that passageway." The lady pointed.

"Oh, Jiao. Yes, I'm sure they're the kind of things she would like." Nora said apprehensively.

"Oh, she did. They were lovely items. A red brass urn with a rose on the side contained a cousin. A ceramic urn contained another cousin, and a nickel urn contained Roy, whoever he was." The woman said, pausing to examine some black Halloween roses in a pot outside the bank.

"Oh, erm…lovely." Nora said, ignoring Ian, a local who dressed up as a skeleton and walked around the town with a large plaque advertising the Castletown Ghost Trail.

They finally reached the car, a small white Skoda.

"Careful. Some ash spilt out of one of the cousin's urns." She warned Nora as she opened her boot.

Nora grimaced.

There were three boxes and a battered yellow plastic tub of books. Nora tentatively began to look through them, keeping a wary eye out for ash. Because it was windy Nora held her breath every time a small gust brushed near in case it scattered the remains of the lady's cousin up her nose.

Two boxes contained theology books including a selection of Bibles. Nora picked some biographies about certain Saints, three of the Bibles, a book of Biblical maps, various apologetic works and some Christian poetry books. Next there was a collection of woodworking books as well as calligraphy tomes. The yellow box contained children's books. Nora chose some classics, a run of Harry Potter's and some Ladybird books.

"I can use these." She told the woman.

"Oh, lovely."

"They would be worth fifteen pounds."

"Sounds good. Thanks. I'll help you carry them back to the shop."

"Thanks." Nora appreciated.

"Hiiiiiii." A familiar voice said next to Nora as the lady closed her boot.

Nora almost dropped the books. She looked over her shoulder to see Harry, a local resident whom The Secondhand Bookworm workers nicknamed The Terminator. He had first arrived dressed all in black with black sunglasses, a crew cut and bulging muscles and said to Nora 'I'll be back' in perfect unwitting imitation of Arnold Schwarzenegger. He had plagued Nora at the bookshop ever since.

Harry was in his running gear; blue running shorts and a tight t-shirt. He was on one of his customary vanity runs, where he jogged around the town past all the female shop keepers with his chest sticking out.

Nora smiled politely.

"Hello, Harry."

"Any new Beano and Dandy annuals?" He asked.

"No, not for a while." Nora replied.

"Are you still with Humphrey?" He then inquired, running on the spot.

"Yes!" Nora said.

"Shame." He grinned and winked. "What are you doing on Saturday?"

"Why?" Nora asked, suspiciously.

"I thought you might like to come to Sheep Dip Farm in Oving. They've got a Horrific Hayride a Creepy Cottage and a Boo Barn to visit with apple bobbing and pigs dressed as witches."

Nora's lips twitched.

"That sounds festive."

"I thought we could ride the Horrific Hayride together." He said.

"No thanks." Nora refused. "I'm working on Saturday and besides, Humphrey would be cross."

"Fair enough." Harry said.

The lady holding the books was looking between Nora and Harry with a smirk. Harry continued jogging on the spot, gazing at Nora.

"Bye." Nora said and set off back towards the bookshop.

"Do you need a hand carrying those?" Harry asked, jogging next to Nora.

"No, I can manage." Nora assured.

"Madam?" Harry offered.

"No thanks." The woman said.

"See you later, Nora." Harry said cheerfully and ran off with his chest sticking out.

The lady looked at Nora, smirking.

When they reached The Secondhand Bookworm Roger was serving a customer. The man had a Homburg hat on his head and wore a tweed suit. The postcard spinners and the black boxes of free paperbacks needed putting out but Roger was having a nice chat while sipping his tea.

"Can we have a pay out of fifteen pounds, please?" Nora asked Roger.

He put his mug of tea down and opened the till, still talking with the man.

"Well yes, you know the problem with drawing lines in the sand? It just takes a breath of air and it blows away." He told the man drearily.

"Quite, quite." The man in the Homburg hat agreed, touched the brim and headed off.

"Fifteen pounds." Roger counted out.

The lady had remained by the door so Nora placed the books she was carrying down on the floor and took the money from Roger to her.

"Thank you, dear." The lady appreciated, passed Nora the last of the books and set off.

A man in an electric wheelchair zoomed up to the door. He pressed a device on his throat.

"Do you have any Agent Pendergast books?" He asked in a robotic voice.

Nora assumed he was using an electrolarynx after having lost his voice box.

"I can have a look for you, sir." Nora offered.

He put on his brakes and sat patiently by the window. Nora hurried back inside.

"I'm just going to check to see if we have any Lincoln Child books for a customer outside." Nora told Roger, putting down the books.

"Your tea's getting cold." He said.

"Oh! I'll be quick."

Nora ran like mad up the stairs, feeling quite dizzy by the time she reached the crime section at the top. She scanned the shelves but couldn't see anything by the author so ran all the way back down.

The man in wheelchair was heading off up the hill. Nora thought he was really impatient.

"No luck!" She called after him.

He stopped, turned around and pressed his throat.

"Thank you for looking." He said robotically and continued away.

With a sigh Nora made her way back to the counter.

"You've been having adventures." Roger smirked, sitting neatly behind the till sipping his tea.

"I'm worn out now." Nora said, plonking down on the stool. She picked up her tea and took a grateful gulp just as a familiar customer arrived with a large black satchel clung over his shoulder.

"Morning." Mr Clegg said.

Mr Clegg often popped in, usually when it was quiet. If there happened to be too many people he would loudly break wind to drive them away. Fortunately the coast was clear.

"Hello, Mr Clegg." Roger greeted.

"Why am I still alive?" He asked himself with a scowl. "And what's with all the decorations? I thought you were too classy to go in for that kind of thing."

"So did I." Roger agreed.

Nora decided to remain quiet so sipped her tea.

"Where's your nuclear war section?" He asked, shuffling along with his bag.

"Erm. We don't have a specific area for nuclear books but our war section is in the back room." Nora said.

"I'll go and have a look." Mr Clegg said and shuffled off down the walkway into the back. "I worked on the atomic bomb." He called over his shoulder.

"What are those books?" Roger asked, pointing to the railway pile.

"Oh. I think Cara dropped them in. They need to go on the shelves."

"I'll do that." Roger decided.

He finished his tea, stood up and began to examine them.

Nora decided to check the emails just as some people arrived.

A plump woman in her sixties with cropped grey hair led an ancient old man into the shop. She proceeded to position him in front of the window. He had a really thick head of grey hair, a long droopy face and a moustache like Hitler's. He looked to be about ninety years of age.

"If my father starts shouting just ignore him. He has dementia." The woman told Nora. "I saw some books in the music section I'd like to buy so I'll leave him here."

Nora stared.

"Oh...okay." She nodded, watching the woman walk off.

Roger headed down the walkway between the front and back rooms with a railway book to put on the shelf, leaving Nora alone with the old man.

"Help me!" The old man said.

Nora looked at him.

"Someone help me!"

He was staring at Nora vacantly.

"Please help me. Help. Help me. HELP ME!"

Nora stood up.

"Is everything okay? What do you need help with?" She asked.

The man looked confused.

"What?" He asked her.

Nora decided not to press the matter.

Slowly the ancient old man smiled.

"Listen to this." He said and cupped his hands together. He then proceeded to clap them gently before his mouth while making shapes with his lips so that the hollow clapping sounded like the English nursery rhyme 'Pop goes the weasel."

Nora stared.

When he had finished he dug his hands into the pockets of his trousers.

"Watch this!" He then said.

He bent his arm and made a small pile of coins on the back of his bent elbow. He held still for a moment and then straightened his arm really quickly, managing to catch all the coins in his hand.

Nora gasped.

Next, he rolled up the newspaper he was holding and held it at both ends with both hands. He then lowered it and before Nora could stop him he jumped over it as if it was a skipping rope. He managed to keep hold of it so he was holding it behind him having never let go. He then took a deep breath.

"Help me. Please help me! Someone help me!" He began to call.

"What is it?" Nora asked quickly.

He looked at her.

"What?" He asked, confused.

"Erm…"

She watched his face break into a smile, he unbuttoned his shirt and stuck his right hand under his left arm pit. He then began to make immensely loud pretend fart noises. They were like an onslaught of small missiles.

The loud pitter-pattering of footsteps came tearing down the stairs.

"Dad!" The woman exclaimed.

The old man stopped.

"I'm so sorry. He has a repertoire of party tricks he used to show the grandchildren." The woman apologised.

"That's alright." Nora said, fighting the laughter bubbling up in her chest.

"Dad! Dad I found you this. You can pay for it dad with your pocket money." The woman called to her father.

He looked confused and lumbered over to the counter.

"It's a pound." The woman told him loudly.

"Eh?" The man asked.

"This book is a pound, dad!" The woman said.

"Eh?" He asked and cupped his hand over his ear.

Roger came back for another railway book to put away. He was smirking.

In the end the woman dug out a pound coin from the man's pockets and placed it in his hand.

"Give the lady the money for your book, dad." She told him.

The old man offered Nora the pound. She went to take it but instead took hold of his finger.

"Oh sorry." She said, glancing down at the pound coin.

She went to take it again but took hold of his finger instead. It was then that she realised he was quickly swapping fingers to tease her.

"Take it then! Take it!" He told her angrily.

"Dad!"

Nora tried to take it but grabbed his finger again. He was very quick. His shoulders shook with laughter. He finally let her take the pound coin.

"Come on then dad. You had sold the music books but this joke book I found on the shelf will keep him amused for hours." The woman told Nora.

"That's great." Nora smiled.

The man placed a wrapped black and white humbug sweet on the open cash book for her and was led off.

"Help me!" He said, stepping up into the street.

Nora looked at Roger. She picked up the sweet.

"Excuse me." A woman called, entering the shop. She wore a witch's hat over blond curls. "Do you have a book about the body in the bread oven at Farleigh Hungerford Castle?"

"Erm…"

"There might not even be a book but I was interested in the story. Apparently Lady Agnes Hungerford burned her husband's body in the castle bread oven after she had murdered him. She wanted to marry Sir Edward Hungerford who was lord of the castle."

"Oh dear." Nora said.

"I visited the castle the other week. There are eight human-shaped lead coffins in a crypt under the chapel too."

Roger stared.

"If we had anything about the castle you could look in our topography section there. We might have some books about castles in architecture too."

"Ah, you probably haven't." The woman said, looking around. "This is a lovely house. Is it your house?"

Nora blinked.

"No I…erm work here."

"Oh how lovely! I have an internet business. I post out sales from EBay. Usually things I find at car boot sales, like toys, net curtains and shapes. It's nice to work from home. Bye."

Nora watched her leave, baffled.

Roger chortled.

"Would you like some pumpkin juice?" He asked. "My treat."

"I think that would be lovely after all these peculiar customers." Nora decided, sitting wearily down in the swivel seat and popping the humbug into her mouth.

"I'll buy us some Halloween themed biscuits too." He decided. "I think we're going to need them."

Nora agreed.

4 FRANKEN-HILL

The pumpkin juice and biscuits in the form of ghosts, monsters and witches went down a treat. Nora and Roger sat behind the counter, chatting and serving customers. Lunchtime arrived quickly and Roger set off promptly at one o'clock, leaving Nora marking up the books she had bought by writing the prices in pencil on the first page in each one. The pile was quickly finished so she continued putting away the railway books because the section was just through the walkway and on bookcases that surrounded the stairs. It was still windy but Nora kept the door open so as not to listen to the door chime all day. Leaves and empty crisp packets floated in and landed on the mat.

"I was accosted by two witches." Roger said, back from his lunch.

Nora bit back a giggle.

"Oh dear."

"One was called Hocus and the other Pocus. They tried to get me to buy Halloween costumes for babies."

"Were they from a shop called 'Kiddies Boutique'?" Nora asked.

"That's right." Roger pulled off his scarf.

"They often walk about the town advertising. One lady did that over Christmas. She came in to sell Christmas babygrows to me." Nora recalled.

"How delightful for you. But I'm more concerned about being accosted by witches." Roger glowered.

Nora chuckled.

"Go and have your lunch now, young lady." Roger said, sitting down in the swivel chair neatly.

"Alright." Nora nodded. "I've priced up the books I bought this morning and put away most of the railway books."

"Thank you for taking my job." Roger smiled sarcastically.

"Sorry, but I wanted something to do."

"Younglings." He sighed, shaking his head and began to read the Skype chat.

Nora retrieved her bag from under the stairs and hurried away into the windy street.

"WHICH MEDIEVAL BEAST ARE YOU?" A man's voice practically shouted in her ear.

Nora yelped.

A man in a medieval costume with a white face, dark rings under his eyes and white powdered hair smiled at her mildly.

"Come to Nineveh House down Market Street and take part in this quiz. Are you a monstrous manticore or are you a gruesome griffin? Are you a wicked wyvern or blood-curdling basilisk? Come along and take our beastly Halloween quiz. You will discover which medieval fantasy beast you are!"

"Oh, no thank you. I'm working today."

The ghostly medieval man bowed and began to follow someone else up the hill, repeating in the same speech.

"Hi, Nora."

Nora stopped at the kerb before crossing the road and saw a lady in a black Victorian costume with a black mourning veil. She jumped.

"Oh. Hello Isla." Nora recognised one of Seymour's actresses. She was handing out leaflets advertising his play 'The Woman in Black' at the Jolly Theatre in Little Cove. "You look brilliant."

"I love this costume." Isla gushed. "And it's fun scaring everyone about Castletown."

"Looking forward to the play?" Nora asked.

"Absolutely. I only get a few moments on stage but I get to act with two famous greats of the English stage. Everyone's admiring how Seymour managed to swipe them from Seatown Festival Theatre."

"Yes. He has his ways." Nora chuckled.

"He sure does." Isla smiled. "When are you coming to see the play?"

"Oh. On Friday." Nora grimaced.

Isla laughed.

"Well, you should be nervous. It's terrifying!" She assured her.

"Thanks." Nora winced.

They said goodbye and Nora headed off to a small café by The Traditional Sweet Shop to the left of the butcher shop on the corner, where she sat and ate a jacket potato and drank a nice pot of tea, surrounded by tombstones, pumpkins and hanging umbrellas with striped witches' legs sticking out of them.

When Nora returned to the shop, Roger was speaking to someone on the telephone.

"Okay, Mr Hill. Yes, I can look now because my colleague is back." He said.

Nora pulled a face.

"I'll take the telephone into the back room now."

Roger pointed towards the walkway. Nora nodded so he set off with the telephone while she placed her bag safely under the staircase behind her.

Mr Hill was a longstanding regular of The Secondhand Bookworm. He telephoned at least once a week to either ask if he could come in to sell his books or to buy them back. He bought and sold the same ten books and had been doing so for about thirty years! Georgina allowed it because she thought it was the only thing that gave Mr Hill a reason to get up in the morning.

Nora heard Roger telling Mr Hill the price of one of his books. She sat down as a Skype chat message arrived.

'Hello Nora and Roger, only me, Betty, what a windy day it is today (and I don't mean me), do you have any books about Little Sea in your Cole section. Customer waiting xx'

Nora typed back:

'Looking now'

She hurried around the counter and checked the section opposite the front door but couldn't see anything specifically about Little Sea. Roger returned, looking grim.

"Mr Hill will be coming over from Seatown in forty five minutes to purchase this book. He called from a phone booth." He said, dropping a black greasy looking copy of a biography about King Charles I onto the cash book.

"Oh how un-delightful." Nora said.

"Use real words, missy." Roger rebuked.

Nora smirked.

"I wonder if he'll arrive on the Gorey-ent Express." She said.

"The what?" Roger frowned.

"The trackless Halloween train that comes up from the station for the festivities."

"Well it would suit him." Roger said.

Nora agreed. She returned to the computer and typed '*no luck, sorry, love Nora xx*' and the telephone began to ring.

Nora and Roger looked at each other. Roger then offered Nora the telephone.

"A punishment for using made up words." He said.

Nora scowled and took the receiver.

"Good afternoon, The Secondhand Bookworm." She said and grimaced to hear an onslaught of heavy breathing.

"Who's that?" Mr Hill's wheezy voice asked.

"It's Nora, Mr Hill." Nora said.

"Norman?" Mr Hill asked.

"NORA!" Nora repeated, offended.

Roger sniggered.

"Norman. I was speaking to a young man just now about a book I would like to purchase." He said.

Nora arched an eyebrow.

"Yes, the Charles I biography." She said.

There was a bout of heavy, rapid breathing, a few splutters.

"It is a biography about King Charles I." He said.

Nora groaned inwardly

"Yes?"

"How much is it?" He asked.

Nora tentatively opened the front cover. Amidst endless pencil marks scrawled over the first page from the hundreds of times Mr Hill had sold the book and bought it back again, was the price.

"It's eight pounds, Mr Hill." Nora said.

"Oh, eight pounds is it? Eight pounds. I see."

"Don't you want it?" Nora asked hopefully.

Coughing and spluttering.

"Oh yes, I would like to purchase the book." Mr Hill assured. He breathed heavily for half a minute. "I'm in a kiosk but I shall be catching the three fifty bus from Seatown. Will you be open today?"

"Yes, we're open now." Nora said.

Mr Hill coughed and breathed heavily for so long that Nora considered hanging up.

"What time do you close?" He finally rephrased.

"Five o'clock." Nora said.

"Oh I shall be there by then. B-bye." He said and hung up.

Nora ground her teeth.

"Would you like a cup of tea?" Roger offered.

Nora sighed.

"Okay, thank you." She accepted.

While Roger was in the kitchen, the Gorey-ent express arrived. Nora stood to watch it unload many passengers in Halloween costumes and then chug past The Secondhand Bookworm, leaving a trail of billowing green smoke in its wake. She smiled and returned to the counter just as a man entered the shop. He closed the door behind him, hard.

"Sorry about that." He apologised, dodging a book that flew off of a shelf in protest. "Do you have a poltergeist?"

He bent down to pick it up.

"It's possible." Nora smiled.

"What's that crying sound?"

Nora froze. He was bent over on the flagstones so her thoughts flew to the supposed well beneath his feet with the body of the young boy wedged down it.

"What crying?" She asked nervously.

"A distant crying. Can't you hear it?"

Nora listened. Sure enough, a distant crying could be heard.

"It sounds like a boy."

Nora stared.

"Oh. It's just that kid." The man then said, looking out the window as he approached the counter.

Nora leaned around him and was relieved to see a local woman pushing a buggy with a crying baby boy having a tantrum while strapped in it. She laughed uneasily.

"Oh. That's a relief."

"No poltergeist then." The man chuckled. "I was wondering if you have a book about the coach made from bones?"

Nora stared.

"The what?"

"The coach made from bones. According to a legend, the ghost of a Lady Howard travels from Okehampton Castle to where she used to live in Tavistock every night at midnight in a coach made from the bones of her former husbands." The man explained.

Nora's eyebrows shot up.

"Hmm, yes, scary stuff." He nodded. "Well, the coach that she travels in is driven by a headless coachman. A pack of skeletal hounds follows behind the coach. Many people believe that Lady Howard has been given the immortal task of removing all the grass from around the castle one blade at a time."

"Goodness." Nora smiled weakly. "That sounds like an old horror movie."

"Oh, I don't know about a movie, but perhaps a book?" He asked.

The telephone began to ring.

"Oh! You can't answer that." The man then said.

"Believe me, I'd rather not." Nora replied, knowing it was Mr Hill.

"No, no. You can't. I'm on the run from the law." He said.

Nora stared.

"Oh. Well, erm. I expect it's just a customer." She assured.

As she reached for the receiver, the man in front of her spun a one hundred and eighty degree turn and bolted for the door. She watched him flee the shop and run up the street, not even batting an eyelid as he passed the zombie who was back walking like the living dead while groaning and handing out leaflets.

"Good afternoon…" She started.

Heavy breathing. A splutter.

"Hello, Mr Hill." Nora sighed.

Coughs, spluttered, rapid breathing and then the sound of the buttons being pushed on the phone keypad. Lots of beeps filled Nora's ear.

"Hello? Hello?" Mr Hill wheezed.

"The Secondhand Bookworm." Nora said flatly.

"Is that The Secondhand Bookworm?"

Roger returned with two mugs of tea. He smirked at Nora.

"Yes, this is The Secondhand Bookworm." Nora said tightly.

"Who's that?" Mr Hill asked.

"It's Nora, Mr Hill."

"Noreen. I have a book put by." Mr Hill said.

Nora decided he was just tormenting her.

"Do you?" She asked innocently.

Coughs, splutters. The sound of breaking wind. Nora closed her eyes.

"Yes. Yes. It's a biography about King Charles II." Mr Hill insisted.

"Oh yes. We have it here."

"Oh, you do. Oh good. Noreen, I shall be catching the bus shortly and will arrive in Castletown at quarter past four. Will you be open?"

"Yes." Nora said wearily.

A woman entered the shop and marched up to the counter. Roger almost choked on his tea.

"You. Do you have a copy of Ant and Bee and the Doctor? It's by Angela Banner. As in Bruce. Bruce Banner? The Hulk." She demanded.

"Oh, you *will* be open will you? Oh, that's good. Good lad. B-bye!" Mr Hill said in Nora's ear and hung up.

Nora was distracted by the woman asking for Ant and Bee.

"We don't get many Ant and Bee books in." Roger told the woman.

"My son loves the Marvel comics and is interested in purchasing them." The woman insisted.

"They have nothing to do with comic books." Roger said.

The woman sniffed frantically.

"Apparently they do. The doctor is Strange or something." She insisted.

"No. Doctor Strange is a Marvel comic hero. So is the Hulk. But the name and the title have nothing to do with Ant and Bee." Roger disagreed.

"You help me dear." The woman turned to Nora.

Roger went red.

"My colleague is correct." Nora nodded. "Ant and Bee are children's books from the 1950's. The author wrote them to help teach her son to read. They're about shapes, days of the weeks, clocks, colours, things like that."

"Hmph. I'll go elsewhere." She said.

Nora and Roger watched her turn around and leave.

Before they could comment, a man who looked like Dudley Moore appeared in the doorway. He was carrying a pumpkin, ready to carve.

"Lots of love." He called into the shop.

Roger choked on his tea again.

Nora stared.

"Pardon?" She asked.

"Lots of love." He repeated, blew her a kiss and continued off up the street.

After a moment, Nora burst out laughing.

"I don't see what there is to laugh about." Roger said grimly.

"I think we've been invaded by ghouls." Nora chuckled and picked up her tea, shaking her head, bemused.

At four thirty, the sound of clonking drew Nora and Roger from their conversation about Margery Kempe. A familiar figure was passing the shop window. Nora stared. Roger paused in mid bite of a custard cream while Nora swallowed the last of Oliver Braithwaite's Halloween fudge with a painful gulp.

Mr Hill had arrived, looking like Frankenstein's Monster. He wore his usual dirty raincoat and carried the same battered green suitcase with a cord cap on his head, covered in medals. But for some reason he was walking like The Monster. When he entered the shop, wheezing and spluttering, Nora noted his shrivelled yellow skin, watery eyes and tight black lips. She looked to see if there were bolts in his neck.

He walked up to the counter without bending his knees, which accounted for the clonking monster-like walk.

"Good afternoon, sir." Mr Hill said cheerfully.

Nora hoped he was speaking to Roger.

"Hello, Mr Hill." Roger smiled glumly.

"I've come from Seatown to purchase a book I've put by. It's priced at eight pounds. It's a biography about King Charles II." Mr Hill said, wheezing as he put his suitcase on the floor.

"Yes, we have it here." Roger said.

"I'll pay by cheque."

"I'll need your cheque card to write your number on the back." Roger reminded him.

"I have it here."

Nora watched Mr Hill retrieve both from the inside of his smelly raincoat. While he waited for Roger to slowly and carefully write his card number on the back of the cheque, he smiled at Nora.

"How are you?" Nora asked.

"Oh, a bit under the weather." He wheezed. He took an enormous dirty hanky out and blew his nose like a trumpet.

"Oh, dear."

"I got osteoarthritis of the knees. They ain't half stiff." He rasped.

"Oh, dear." Nora repeated again, leaning back to avoid bogies.

"All done, Mr Hill. Do you need a bag?" Roger asked, passing Nora the cheque to place in the till.

"No thank you, son." Mr Hill shook his head and hoisted up his suitcase. He paused to look at a book displayed. It was a hardback copy of 'Frankenstein' by Mary Shelley. Nora swallowed back a giggle.

Once the biography was in his case he jabbed a finger in the direction of Roger.

"All the best! I'm very satisfied with my transaction." He said.

"Thank you, Mr Hill." Roger said politely.

"Good luck, lad." Mr Hill told Roger. He ignored Nora and set off, walking like Frankenstein's Monster once more.

Nora grimaced.

"I expect he'll be on the phone trying to resell that one tomorrow. First thing." Roger sighed.

Nora popped the cheque in the till.

"I hope he calls Seatown."

"Thanks a bunch."

"You're welcome." Nora said and they went back to discussing Margery Kempe.

At the end of the day they turned the upstairs lights off and locked up after bringing the objects in from outside. It had been a slow day with takings only reaching two hundred and sixty pounds. Nora was counting out the float and Roger was about to shut and lock the door when a man stuck his head in the door. Roger yelped.

"Any Muffin the Moo?" He shouted at Nora.

She dropped several coins.

"Oh. No, I'm afraid no…" She began.

"Na, na, na. Na. Na, na, na. One day, one day." The man interrupted and walked off.

Roger shut the door and locked it fast.

"One of your customers, no doubt." He scowled.

"He comes when there's a craft fair in the scout hut. He collects books about Muffin the Mule."

"Are there any?" Roger asked.

"Yes. I found 'Meet Muffin the Mule' for him once. Just a tatty copy with no dust wrapper. And I came across 'Muffin and the Magic Hat' on someone's book shelf once, but the woman wouldn't sell it."

"Funny." Roger scoffed, shrugging into his coat. "Well, it has been delightful working with you again."

"Now I live in Castletown we can't car pool anymore."

"Well that suits me." Roger said.

Nora saw him smirking.

"Yes, I had enough of your carbon emissions." She sighed.

He laughed.

They finished packing up, said '*byeeeeeee*' to Seatown via Skype chat, turned off the computer and the lights and set the alarm. Roger waited by the open door and Nora ran around the counter and out of the shop.

"What are your plans tonight?" Nora asked Roger as he locked the door.

"I'm going to my daughter's house for dinner. Afterwards we're playing trains."

"Trains?" Nora asked, imagining Roger driving a miniature steam train around his daughter's back garden.

"It's a game with dominoes."

"Oh, that's nice."

"Yes. What about you?"

"Humphrey is coming over at seven thirty to take me to the town hall. They're showing old scary silent black and white movies." She said with a wince. "He loves silent horror movies."

"Don't get too scared." Roger smirked.

"I'll try not to!" Nora assured him.

He turned and headed off in the opposite direction to Nora's flat.

"Speak to you tomorrow, no doubt." He called.

"Thank you for the biscuits."

"My pleasure." He smiled, gave a small wave and Nora watched him walk away.

With a smile she checked the shop door was locked, noticed the Red Plaque on the wall next to the window, shuddered and quickly began home, wondering what horrible nightmares she would have after an evening watching 'The Cabinet of Dr Caligari' and 'The Phantom Carriage' in the old town hall.

5 PRIDE AND PREJUDICE AND WEREWOLVES

Wednesday morning was wet and windy. The rain pelted the windows and the wind blew leaves in eddies in the corners of Nora's back garden. She peered down upon the iron table and chairs in the middle of the flagstones, surrounded by two sides of ancient stone walls from the Duke's estate and the wall of the unused garden next door. A rook from the castle was standing in the centre of the table, staring at her. Nora yanked her curtain aside quickly and ran out of her bedroom.

She had had an unnerving evening with Humphrey at the town hall. The movies had given her the heebie-jeebies. 'The Cabinet of Dr Caligari' was a German film and had been released in 1919. The plot was about an insane and mysterious hypnotist who kept a somnambulant locked in a closet. He would then send the somnambulant off on errands of death to commit murders. It was actually set in an insane asylum. The music was unnerving and the sets surreal, with sharp points, shadows and streaks of light, the latter of which were painted on the sets. Nora had been wary of her wardrobe all night in case a noctambulist emerged.

'The Phantom Carriage' had followed. It was a Swedish horror film released in 1921 about a death carriage. The last person to die each year was destined to drive the phantom carriage and collect the souls of everyone who died the following year. It was New Year's Eve and David was whacked on the head with a bottle just as the clock struck twelve. A series of flashbacks followed and David regained consciousness in time to stop a woman dying of consumption from poisoning her children! The double exposure effects for the ghost carriage were effective and realistic. In the darkness of the town hall Nora had been so absorbed that Humphrey had made her shriek when he had offered her some popcorn in the darkness.

After a quick breakfast and after feeding 'Beardie', her pet lizard, his crickets, Nora grabbed her bag and ran down the stairs. She stepped into her wellies, shrugged on her mac and opened her front door just as a car drove past and sent a puddle sailing through the air. Fortunately it didn't reach her so she put up her umbrella, closed and locked her door, and set off down the steep hill to The Secondhand Bookworm.

Nora was standing in front of a small bakery several shops away from The Secondhand Bookworm, gazing at a row of large iced buns some moments later, when a familiar figure squashed himself under her umbrella.

"Eeeeep! Hee-loo Nora." A recognisable voice said.

She looked at the greasy round head next to her and almost let go of the handle so her umbrella nearly sailed away.

"White-Ligh…." She started and stuttered. "I mean…Joe?!" She corrected, surprised.

"Yep. Long-time no…eeeeeeek."

Nora assumed he was about to say 'see', but water was trickling off her umbrella and down his neck. He sidled closer to her and gazed up miserably.

Joe had been a regular customer at The Secondhand Bookworm until he had been caught stealing books. He had had a run of bad luck and after being made redundant had become addicted to his favourite brand of cider, White Lightning, the same name that the workers in The Secondhand Bookworm had given Joe as his moniker years before.

White-Lightning Joe was an odd little man with strange mannerisms and black oily hair. He had left Castletown after being caught stealing books from the shelves in the Cole section of The Secondhand Bookworm and selling them back to the shop as his own. His mugshot was currently on the wall leading under the stairs.

"Nora. Am I still banned?" He asked sadly.

Nora edged away from him.

"Oh. Yes, I expect so." Nora nodded.

"But it's been ages! I've done my time." He insisted. His bottom lip trembled. "What can I do to make Georgina forgive me? Would you put in a good word for me, Nora?"

"Erm…alright. I'll ask her." Nora nodded.

"Oh you would?! Eeeeeeee!" He exclaimed, pleased. "Nora. Can you lend me two quid?"

"You know I can't lend customers money."

"I'm hardly a customer. I'm banned for thievery!" He insisted enthusiastically.

"I can't lend money to…er…past bookshop thieves." She assured, beginning to edge away.

"Oh." His shoulders slumped. "Ooookaaaaay." He sighed.

He emerged into the pelting rain as Nora continued edging away from him with her umbrella, but he didn't seem to notice. He stood getting soaked, looking miserable.

"Well, I'd better go and open up the shop." She told him.

He looked up, gave a small wave and slumped off. Nora turned and fled.

When she reached the bookshop she saw her colleague Agnes squashed in the corner by the door with a plastic carrier bag on her head. Nora almost skidded over.

"Morning!" Nora said, digging out her keys.

"Hi, Nora." Agnes smiled, biting into a carrot. "I see the road is flooding."

Nora glanced over her shoulder. Water running down the steep hill was collecting outside The Secondhand Bookworm in the road just beyond the pavement outside the door. In the past, these great puddles had been the cause of flooding in the front of the shop, but with the new door and step the shop was now waterproof. However, it didn't stop *people* from getting wet. Whenever a car drove through the puddle it made a four foot wave. Woe betide anyone standing in front of the door when that happened.

"Car!" Nora exclaimed, seeing one hurtling down the hill towards them.

"Bonanza!" Agnes said grimly, pulling her carrier bag further down her forehead.

Nora managed to unlock the door and they both jumped inside just as the car reached the road in front of the shop. Agnes slammed the door just in time. A large wave hit the window.

"Perfectly sealed." She said as Nora dropped her open umbrella on the flagstones and ran to turn off the alarm.

"Thank goodness." Nora sighed.

Agnes turned the key that Nora had passed her for the door so they had some time to set up for the day before any customers arrived.

"Ooooh I love the decorations." Agnes smiled, tugging off her plastic bag to reveal her riot of red curls.

"Great, aren't they?" Nora nodded, giving the bag a curious look.

"Oh. I don't have an umbrella or a rain hat so I thought this would do. My hair is lovely and dry." Agnes explained, finishing off her carrot and stuffing the plastic bag into her rucksack. "If it gets wet I look like an old lady with a fresh, tight perm."

Nora laughed.

"How's university?" Nora asked as she took off her mac. Agnes studied medicine in Nottingham but during holidays and half terms she came home to her family's house outside Castletown. Georgina always gave her a few days' work at the bookshop.

"Oh. Fine." Agnes nodded. "I did faint though. We went on a field trip to a local hospital and when the nurse gave someone an injection I passed out."

"Oh dear. Are you still going to be a doctor?"

"Why not." Agnes shrugged and began to hum as she crossed the room.

She didn't have a coat on but was just in a yellow jumper and black skater skirt with brown tights and small boots. Agnes always seemed oblivious to the elements. So she just popped her rucksack under the stairs and passed Nora the cash float.

Nora filled up the till and once Agnes had turned on the light for the floors above them and checked for any roof leaks (there were none), they arranged the postcard spinners out of the way inside by the window and opened up.

Nora closed her umbrella and squashed it behind the door, ignoring the two-tone door chime as she left the door open.

"Ugh. What a wet day." She said.

"Do you think we'll have any customers?" Agnes mused.

"I expect so."

"What's the plan for today?"

"Well. We could just tidy up some sections if we get bored." Nora said. "There haven't been any deliveries of books to put away yet."

"Okay." Agnes nodded. "Let's hope the rain stops soon."

"I expect it will." Nora was optimistic.

She noticed that the rain was coming in the opened doorway so reluctantly closed it.

"I'm looking forward to the play." Agnes said, picking up a new copy of 'The Woman in Black' from the counter.

"Hmm." Nora said warily.

Agnes began to read it so Nora turned on the computer and checked the telephone to see if anyone had left a message. There were none.

The haunted Tuk-Tuk trundled past. A bloodcurdling scream told Nora that a text message had arrived on her phone.

"What was that?" Agnes looked up.

"Oh, just my phone." Nora said and read the text. It was from Humphrey, asking if she had been able to sleep after watching the horror movies in the town hall. Nora quickly replied that she had imagined a somnambulant emerging from her wardrobe and that a rook had been giving her the evil eye that morning.

'Are you still on for tonight? xx' Humphrey asked

'Another evening of terror? Xx ' Nora replied.

Agnes grinned at the frequent blood-curdling screams.

'The Ghost Trail followed by dinner and a play in the dungeons. So, yes. Xx.' He replied.

Nora chuckled.

'I think I'm seeing too much of you. You may get the wrong idea. Xx' She sent.

'I know you love me.' Humphrey replied.

Nora smiled and sent back a row of kisses.

A man under an umbrella walked past the window and pushed open the door.

"Cuckoo-cuckoo." He said in imitation to the two-toned chime.

Nora recognised Spencer, one of her regular customers, who had popped in to the bookshop already that week on Monday. He wore his customary long black coat, like a vampire cape.

"Hello." Nora greeted, warily.

"Morning." Spencer said, closing his umbrella as he shut the door behind him. "What a dreadful morning."

"Yes. Very wet." Nora agreed.

"Do you have anything about the Unseen Hands of Bolsover Castle?" Spencer asked, gliding to the counter.

"Er...no. That sounds scary."

"I'm going there again at the weekend. The last time I went I came across Sir Charles Cavendish himself." Spencer said.

"As a ghost?" Nora asked.

"Yes, of course. He's been dead a few centuries now. He's a ghost, or a troubled spirit caught between our worlds."

Agnes turned a page in The Woman in Black, seemingly oblivious to Spencer.

"It's an amazing place and many spirits roam the corridors and the grounds. The empty riding school has the supernatural smell of horses lingering." Spencer said.

"Lovely."

"The best things about it all are the invisible pinches and slaps given by unseen hands. I received several on my last trip. It was amazing." Spencer said dreamily.

Nora's eyes widened.

"You actually felt a slap?"

"Right across my face. And my arm was pinched twice."

Nora supposed Spencer had been in his element with such horrors.

"So I was hoping there was a book about it."

"I've never seen anything specific." Nora assured.

"Ah. That's a shame."

"Would you like me to look online to see if there is anything printed?"

"No, don't worry; I can do that at home. I want to write an article about it for the December issue of the international esoteric magazine 'Apocrypha'. One of many I contribute to." He said. "Hopefully I'll receive some more pinches and slaps at the weekend. I'll tell you all about it when I get back."

Nora grimaced.

"You missed a great 'magic potion forage' last night." He said and then noticed the book Agnes was reading. "Ah, 'The Woman in Black'. My wife and I have tickets to your brother's play on Friday night. We're bringing Mal."

"I'm sure you'll all enjoy it. It's supposed to be terrifying." Nora nodded.

"Can't wait." Spencer smirked. "I'll buy a copy of that."

Nora smiled and watched him take one from the window display. He said he would read it when he got home, paid, bade them goodbye, picked up his umbrella and set off in the rain with 'The Woman in Black' tucked safely in his vampire cape. Nora and Agnes looked at one another and Agnes grinned.

It wasn't until eleven o'clock that Nora and Agnes had their first customers of the day. Two elderly men entered The Secondhand Bookworm with dripping umbrellas which they shook out into the street and placed behind the door. One of the men was short with black hair and enormous glasses. The other was large and plump with white hair and black horn-rimmed glasses. They reminded Nora of The Two Ronnies.

"They look like The Two Ronnies." Nora whispered to Agnes.

"The who?"

"You've never heard of The Two Ronnies?!"

"No. Are they criminals?"

Nora suppressed a giggle.

"No. They were a comedy due from the 1980's. They had a TV show."

"Are you saying we look like the two Ronnies?" The smaller man asked.

Nora jumped.

"Oh…er….well…actually, I was." Nora admitted sheepishly.

"We do, don't we!" The larger man joined in.

"Do you sell fork handles?" The smaller man asked.

Nora laughed.

Agnes looked confused.

"Four candles! No, fork handles!" The larger man said.

Nora continued to laugh, while Agnes looked even more confused.

"You'll have to look on Youtube for some of their TV clips." Nora told her as the Two Ronnies wandered off for a browse.

Agnes decided to do so there and then. She discovered a Two Ronnies sketch titled 'the confusing bookshop' and so they watched it with the sound low, laughing and giggling as Ronnie Corbett tried to locate a book in a bookshop run by Ronnie Barker which had been organised into sections by colour of book throughout the shop.

When the Two Ronnies returned from their browse they purchased several bags of various books.

"It's goodbye from him." The smaller man grinned.

"And it's goodbye from me!" The large man said.

Nora and Agnes laughed and the men left cheerfully.

"I know I shall be binge watching all these videos tonight." Agnes decided.

"You'll enjoy them." Nora knew.

The rain had eased off and it looked as though the sun was coming out. People were emerging into the town like snails.

A woman dressed as a werewolf pushed open the door.

Nora and Agnes looked up and stared.

"Hello." The werewolf greeted.

She wore a foam latex werewolf head prosthetic over the top part of her face which had black and grey wolf hair, scary yellow eyes, a wolf nose and large hairy wolf ears. Her hands were hairy claws, she wore tattered skinny jeans, a t-shirt and a red and black tattered check blouse open but with the hem gathered and tied in a knot at her waist.

"Morning." Nora greeted faintly.

"Hi! We have a Jane Austen book club and we're going to read Pride and Prejudice next." The werewolf said.

"The 'Werewolves Jane Austen Book Club'?" Nora asked.

Agnes giggled.

"Yes." The werewolf laughed. "We're actually in the town for the next couple of days advertising the Duke's Halloween Ball taking place at the castle on Thursday night. Are you coming along?"

"I am." Nora nodded, trying not to sound too keen, though her heart betrayed her and skipped a beat. She had had a crush on the Duke of Cole ever since he had visited the bookshop last Christmas when the town had been closed during to immense snowfall. He had invited her to a private tour of his personal library over the summer and was collecting First Edition P G Wodehouse books after Nora had given him one as a gift.

"Oh that's wonderful. Are you?" The werewolf asked Agnes.

"No." Agnes smiled.

"Well, we're from the Duke's castle events planning committee and as all of us belong to a book club too. So you will be getting requests from a lot of werewolves today for copies of Pride and Prejudice."

"We probably have about three or four new Wordsworth edition copies in stock and perhaps some secondhand copies in the attic room on the top floor." Nora said.

"Oh, are there more floors?" The werewolf asked, amazed.

"Yes. The staircase is back there."

"Oh I must have a quick look. How wonderful." She said, making her way to the walkway.

"Wordsworth editions are on the next floor staircase, you can't miss them. They will be in alphabetical order of author. The paperback fictions room in right up the top, as far as you can go, and in the attic." Nora explained.

"Thanks! Up I go." The werewolf said and disappeared.

"You're going to the Duke's Halloween Ball?" Agnes asked Nora.

"Yes, Humphrey and I are going. It's for a charity called 'Aid to the Church in Need'. The Duke of Cole is a Catholic." Nora nodded.

"Is it fancy dress?"

"Yes." Nora smiled. "You need separate tickets for the dinner in the Earl's Hall. The ball takes place afterwards and is open to everyone."

"Sounds nice." Agnes said.

"I'm quite excited about it." Nora admitted dreamily.

"Is it a costume ball?"

"Yes."

"What are you going as?"

"Well, I have my Ghostly Lady costume to wear to work on Saturday and at first I thought about wearing that to the ball. But then I found an amazing costume – the vampire ghost of Queen Elizabeth I. It's a billowing Elizabethan dress with a large Elizabethan neck ruff and a tall wig of red curls with a pair of vampire fangs. Humphrey has the vampire ghost of Sir Francis Walsingham costume. They are much more befitting the Duke of Cole, so we're going as those."

"That sounds awesome." Agnes admired. "Are you sure vampires can be ghosts?"

"No. I don't think so. Vampires are corporeal but ghosts aren't. I think vampires are immortal and live about 1000 years. Ghosts are the souls of the dead, caught between worlds. Yes, I read a lot of the books that come in for sale here and Cara is a ghost and vampire expert. But a ghost and a vampire rolled into one sounded too good to pass up." Nora grinned.

"It sounds bonanza! Take some photos." Agnes chuckled.

"I will." Nora assured. "The costumes are at my parents' house in Little Cove so I shall be getting ready there."

A man arrived. He wore a rich orange t-shirt that had 'Psyche Ward' printed on it with a number underneath. Nora raised her eyebrow.

"Do you have the latest crime novel by…I can't remember his name but he looks like that actor, Chris O'Donnell. You know, the one who was in that movie 'Vertical Limit' where he had to rescue a group of people including his sister in an avalanche."

Agnes stared, mesmerized.

"Yes!" Nora then exclaimed.

They both looked at her.

"I remember that film." She said, pleased.

"What's the author's name? He writes crime about missing persons."

"Oh. Do you mean Tim Weaver?"

The man snapped his fingers and pointed at Nora.

"That's him."

Agnes was impressed.

"Well if we did have anything by him it would be on the top floor."

"Gulp." The man said.

Agnes stood up.

"Shall I look for you?" She offered.

"You can lead the way and then leave me to browse." The man decided and they set off.

The telephone started to ring.

"Good morning, The Secondhand Bookworm." Nora said politely.

"It's me." Georgina's cheerful voice replied. "How's it going?"

"The rain's eased off." Nora said.

"Good. You should get some customers then. Can you do a pay-out for me please? If you write it in the cash book and put the money in an envelope and pop it under the tray with your twenty pound note excess I'll pick it up on my way through tonight."

"Of course." Nora nodded and picked up a pen.

"One hundred and ninety five pounds, Mr Coats, Little Sea."

"That'll clear us out of money."

"Sorry." Georgina apologised.

"Okay, I've written it down."

"Thank you. You're going to the Duke's Halloween Ball on Thursday evening aren't you?"

"How funny. A werewolf just asked me the same thing."

Georgina fell silent.

Nora sniggered.

"Mad town." Georgina finally said. "Troy thinks he might want to go after all. So we're in Piertown looking at costumes."

"Oh that will be nice." Nora smiled.

"Did you hear that Felix and Roger just had a famous customer?"

"No. Who?"

"Oh, I can't remember his name. Some English actor. Apparently he had baked bean sauce all down his front."

"Oh dear."

"Yes. He's performing in Seatown Festival Theatre for the autumn. Felix said he was complaining about The Jolly Theatre probably pinching his audience."

Nora laughed.

"Cara was cross she missed him. She's in the office doing the accounts."

"By the way. Guess who I ran into this morning?" Nora remembered.

"Who?" Georgina asked with suspicion.

"White-Lightning Joe."

"Oh that horrid little man! I hope he didn't try to come into the bookshop!"

"No. But he wanted me to ask you if he is still banned."

"Yes he is!" Georgina assured wrathfully. "Don't let him in, Nora."

"Alright. I promise." Nora assured.

"The cheek! Hang on. Pardon, darling? No I don't mind wearing suspenders." She called out.

Nora smothered a laugh.

"I'd better go before Troy choses me an embarrassing get-up for the ball. Oh, I meant to ask, are you still on for spooky readings in the bookshop on Saturday?"

"I'd forgotten about that!" Nora exclaimed.

"Cara put a poster up in the Seatown shop to advertise it. You can put one in the window there. Lots of people will be interested. It'd be a good Shriek-Week event for the shop."

"Okay." Nora sighed.

"You'll be wonderful at it, Nora." Georgina assured. "I expect I will hear lots of compliments about you afterwards."

"Alright. For the sake of the compliments." Nora decided cheerfully.

"Thank you, Nora. Agh. Troy's trying on a corset. I'd better go. Have a good day."

"Bye." Nora chuckled.

When she had replaced the telephone receiver she placed the pay-out cash into an envelope and lamented the empty till which was now just full of coins and a few fivers. The werewolf returned, bought a copy of Pride and Prejudice in Wordsworth edition and left. Nora ordered a replacement copy from their new book supplier online. She then checked her watch and decided that she and Agnes should do lunch shortly. While Agnes was still upstairs, Nora Skyped Seatown and asked if Cara could send her the Spooky Reading poster. Felix sent it through.

'We're working together on Saturday. I won't have to read anything will I!?' Felix asked.

'No, don't worry. It'll just be me.' Nora grimaced.

Georgina had roped Nora into agreeing to read excerpts from a selection of children's books on Saturday which was Halloween. Nora had chosen to read from an Edward Gorey tome such as 'The Gashlycrumb Tinies' because she liked his illustrations. It was rather selfish of her because only she would see the drawings as she read, but the stories were grim and entertaining too. The readings would take place between noon and one o'clock in the children's room. Nora thought it would give her a nice break from serving customers and it would be fun to scare some children.

She printed out the poster that Cara had made and stuck it on the window of the door.

Agnes returned with the customer looking for the latest Tim Weaver books. He was carrying an armful of novels.

"We couldn't find any Tim Weaver but I can't resist all these." He told Nora.

She smiled, moving aside for Agnes to take the sale.

Another werewolf appeared. It opened the door and stood on the doorstep.

"Grrrr." He said.

"Pride and Prejudice?" She asked.

The werewolf gave a start.

"How did you know?!"

Nora thought it was amusing to see a flabbergasted werewolf.

"One of your book club friends has already been in."

"Oh." The werewolf chuckled. "I don't mind what state the book is in. The cheaper the better."

"I'll run up and grab all the copies we have." Nora decided. "Back in a moment."

When she came back down carrying seven paperback editions of Pride and Prejudice, the werewolf was pondering a selection of Penguin book mugs that were displayed.

"I'm tempted with these. Four for thirty six quid? That's good. Do you always have them in stock?"

"Yes." Nora nodded.

"I'll come back when I'm not dressed like a lycanthrope." He said.

"Okay." Nora smiled.

He chose the cheapest copy of Jane Austen's classic, retrieved a wallet from amongst his fur and took it off cheerfully. Nora turned to Agnes.

"We should do lunches." She said.

"Good idea. Would you like to go first?"

"I can if you don't mind."

"No, I don't mind at all. Go ahead." Agnes nodded, sitting down in the swivel chair. "While it's quiet I'll watch some Two Ronnies."

Nora laughed, grabbed her bag and set off into the damp.

6 IN THE DUNGEONS

Nora popped into the delicatessen on the corner just across the road outside The Secondhand Bookworm. Alice and Philip ran the shop which was full of choice cheeses, cigars, expensive wine, delicious homemade sandwiches, pastries, jars of jams and pickles, fresh bread and vegetables and endless other delights. It was beautifully decorated for Halloween inside.

"Afternoon, Nora." Philip greeted, looking up from filling up a large dish of olives.

"Hello."

"Busy in the bookshop?"

"Quiet today." Nora replied, examining a variety of Turkish delight.

"Yes, it's been quiet here." He nodded.

Alice emerged with a carved pumpkin.

"Hello, Nora." She smiled.

"Hello, Alice. Are you serving jacket potatoes?"

"Certainly." She nodded, popping the pumpkin on the counter. It smiled at Nora evilly.

"Thanks. With tuna and mayonnaise, please?" Nora asked, glaring at the pumpkin.

"Lovely." Alice smiled.

The potatoes had been baked that morning and were kept in a warming drawer. It was ready for her in minutes and she took it back to The Secondhand Bookworm to eat in the kitchen.

Agnes was dealing with a customer.

"Do you sell keyrings that answer when you whistle?" The man was asking Agnes.

"Not here." Agnes replied.

"Oh. Where are your free books?" He next asked.

"All of our books are for sale." Agnes said, glancing at Nora.

Nora paused, holding her dish of potato. The man looked at it.

"Is that a potato? Have you never read 'The Spud from Outer Space'?" He demanded. "Potatoes are *evil*. Preachers used to lecture about the ills of potatoes. Not only are they related to the deadly nightshade, which is linked to devils and witches, but they encourage idleness." He quoted.

Nora's lips twitched.

"Well, the more we eat then the less potatoes there will be in the world." She said, humouring him.

"Tell me, have you got any books by thingy?"

"Thingy?"

"I can't remember his name."

"No, sorry."

"Is Mr Bookworm here?"

"Who?"

"The owner of the shop."

Nora wanted to giggle.

The door opened and the man turned at the sound of the door chime. Nora gave a start to see White-Lightning Joe standing on the threshold.

"Heeeelope." He said, looking sheepish.

The man bowed to Agnes.

"Thank you for your time. I have an appointment at the gynaecologist." He said and dashed off.

Agnes grinned.

White-Lightning Joe moved aside for the crazy man and almost fell into the shop.

"Oooops. He he he." He said and balanced on the step. "Did you speak to Georgina?"

"Yes. I'm afraid you're still banned."

White-Lightning Joe's bottom lip began to tremble.

"Oh that sucks!" He lamented drearily. "I've served my sentence. Can't I come in, Nora?"

"No." Nora said firmly. "You were stealing books and selling them back to us. It's almost an unforgivable sin to the bookseller."

"I've converted." He insisted.

"Sorry." Nora said.

He sighed loudly.

"Eeeep." He shrugged. "I'm still unemployed. Nora. Do you think there's a job for me at your brother's theatre? I used to work in the theatre, yay!"

Nora thought about that. Seymour had said he was looking for someone who had experience to work behind the scenes. And her brother had a soft heart.

"I can ask him." She consented.

White-Lightning Joe's eyes lit up.

"Oh would you? Thanks, Nora. Thanks. Thank you! Thanks." He gave a small wave. "I'll come to the door again and you can let me know what he says."

"Okay." Nora sighed.

He gave a frantic wave, turned and headed off.

Agnes smiled.

"Mind if I go and eat this spud from outer space?" Nora grinned.

"Go ahead." Agnes chuckled and Nora headed off for the kitchen for a bit of peace!

Agnes finished at four o'clock and set off into the growing darkness. They had wheeled one of the postcard spinners onto the pavement for the afternoon, but hadn't sold a single one. Apart from a trade customer spending two hundred pounds on a set of leather books that Nora had displayed on the counter, as well as several people purchasing books from the Halloween display window and three more werewolves buying copies of Pride and Prejudice for their book club, takings had been slow and customers almost non-existent.

The Gorey-ent Express had chugged into town again and deposited two carriages full of people in costumes, but they had headed off to various pubs and a circus tent that had been erected up at the folly in the Duke's park estate. Apparently there was an evening of haunted folly tours, talks and spooky readings up there, followed by a séance.

As she sat reading her Kindle for the last hour, Nora became aware of terrible, out of tune singing accompanied by the strumming of a guitar. She looked up to see the form of a vampire crossing the square. He crooned all the way across the cobles, eyes fixed on the bookshop and once he reached it threw open the door.

"Then you can mash
Then you can monster mash
The monster mash
And do my graveyard smash
Then you can mash
You'll catch on in a flash
Then you can mash
Then you can monster mash." He sang in conclusion, grinning and showing his missing teeth. He then bowed low.

Nora recognised him from Christmas when he had plagued Castletown dressed as a scruffy Saint Nicholas singing out of tune carols.

"Oh. Hello." She said, warily.

"How about another?" He asked and before she could reply he began to strum. One of his guitar strings snapped and twanged about for a moment but he ignored it.

"How d' you do I
See you've met my
Faithful handyman
He's just a
Little brought down because
When you knocked
He thought you were the candy man." The vampire-hobo started to sing.

Nora grimaced.

"I'm just a sweet transvestite." He crooned.

Nora's eyes widened. She thought she had better persuade him not to sing her the entire repertoire from The Rocky Horror Picture Show so stood up.

"I'm sorry but I'm closing the shop." She fibbed.

He stopped strumming and stared.

"Oh that's a shame luv. How 'bout a donation for the songs?" He asked and held out his hand.

"Sorry but I'm not allowed to give donations." She said lamely.

He cackled.

"One of them is you?" He said, turned around and set off, continuing his song in the street.

Nora winced.

A zombie walker began to stagger past the shop with his leaflets advertising the town zombie walks. Nora dived under the counter.

When the door opened again she peered over the top of the counter and sighed with relief to see her brother and sister.

"What are you doing?" Heather giggled, stepping into the room.

"Avoiding a toothless singing vampire-hobo." Nora said, standing up.

Heather laughed.

"Did you know there are zombies outside?" Milton asked, closing the door behind him.

"Yes." Nora grimaced.

"I love this town." He said.

"We're here early and thought we'd keep you company. Are you on your own?" Heather asked, peering around at the decorations.

"Agnes left at four." Nora nodded.

"Cara and Seymour said they'll be here at six. We can get drinks in the haunted pub down Market Street while we wait. What time is Humphrey arriving?" Heather asked.

"He'll be here anytime." Nora smiled.

"Apparently Castletown Museum is advertising itself as 'The Creepiest Museum in Cole'." Milton said, picking up a book. "They have rooms of portraits of ghosts with no eyes or with moving eyes."

"That's horrible." Nora grimaced.

"I like the pile of human bones in your window." Milton then grinned.

"Mind if I go and have a browse?" Heather asked.

"Go ahead. I'll close up in about fifteen minutes. I'll hold out until five just in case we have a last minute big spender."

While her brother and sister disappeared and creaked about the stairs and upper floors, Nora answered the telephone.

"Good afternoon, The Secondhand Bookworm." She said.

"Hi Nora, it's me." Georgina replied.

"Hi!"

"How's it been?"

"Very slow."

"Bah. Hopefully the rest of the week will pick up. I've chosen a costume for the ball."

"Have you? What are you going as?" Nora smiled.

"Mrs Lovett. Troy is going as Sweeny Todd."

Nora laughed.

"I can't wait to see you both." She said.

"They're a little bit gory but Troy loves them. About tomorrow. I'll pick you up from the bookshop after ten."

"Oh yes, calls." Nora sighed.

"Hmm. Well we only have five so we'll end up back at the shop to unload for you to do some pricing the following day. And then I'll drop you home to Little Cove."

"Thanks." Nora appreciated.

"Betty and Cara are in Castletown tomorrow so leave them any instructions you can think of."

"Okay." Nora said and thought hard.

"Right, I'd better call Seatown. Before you go tonight, can you do a stock check of Wordsworth editions and send it through to Felix please?"

"No problemo. How has Felix been today?"

"I'm going to find out now." Georgina said sternly. "Hopefully he hasn't made any more mistakes."

"Ah well, we all make them." Nora said.

"I suppose." Georgina sighed. "See you tomorrow."

"Bye." Nora bade and they rang off.

She enlisted the help of Milton and Heather with the Wordsworth edition stock check and sent them off with a list each; Heather to check A-J and Milton to check K-Z. While they were doing that Nora tried to think of some tasks for Betty and Cara but gave up. She then had a couple of last minute customers.

"Your doorway is too small." One man, with a face like a hippo, said.

"Oh, sorry about that." Nora apologised.

He bought a book from the window and left.

"Does the Duke live at the castle?" A woman dressed as Wednesday from The Addams Family asked.

"Yes." Nora replied.

"He must be ancient."

"No, he's only in his early thirties."

"Bet he's crooked." The woman said and walked out.

A man in a crocodile costume bought some postcards. A lady dressed as the Irish female pirate Anne Bonny (so she said) picked up a free map and said that the pumpkin candles in the window were dangerous and could cause a fire. She then spent forty pounds on a couple of folio society books, one Observer and an art book and left.

Nora was thankful when she finally wheeled in the postcard spinner and turned the sign to 'CLOSED' just as Humphrey arrived.

"Evening." He smiled, stepping down into the shop.

"Hello." Nora smiled back.

She locked up and sighed in relief.

"That was a weird day."

"Every day here is a weird day." Humphrey smirked, wheeling the postcard spinner onto the carpet with the other.

"I agree." Nora chuckled. "Heather and Milton are here. They're just doing a Wordsworth stock list check for me. Seymour and Cara will be over by six."

"Cool." Humphrey helped Nora cash up.

When Heather and Milton came down, Heather had turned off the upstairs light and read out the stock for Nora to fill in on the computer. She then saved the file and sent it through to Seatown.

'Thanks! See you soon xxx Cara.' Cara replied.

Heather chatted with her for a while until they were ready to go to the haunted pub, shut down the computer, turned off the light, set the alarm and legged it.

The haunted pub had even more fake cobwebs than The Secondhand Bookworm. According to the Red Plaque on the wall outside twelve witches were hanged directly in front of the building in 1618 and their spirits walked into the pub over Halloween. If you were lucky you could sit and have a drink with them.

Humphrey bought a round of 'Spooky Sunrise' cocktails and they sat at the bar surrounded by witches, wizards, mummies, aliens and all the werewolves from 'The Jane Austen Werewolf Book Club' while listening to 'Black Magic Woman' by Fleetwood Mac on a loop until Seymour and Cara finally arrived.

Cara had booked a table in the dungeon for a meal and to watch the performance that was apparently on in there, but first they were going to go on the Ghost Trail. They squeezed out of the pub onto the street and made their way along the busy sidewalk. Castletown was lively in the evening with ghost stories being read in select houses, the Haunted history trail taking place until ten o'clock and the party up by the folly. Several zombies were hulking about groaning.

"We should stay open until midnight." Cara said, stepping around an evil clown that was vomiting in the gutter.

"Eeeew. Not the sort of customers I'd like to serve." Nora objected.

"Is that White-Lightning Joe?" Heather pointed out.

They all looked in the direction of her finger. Sure enough, White-Lightning Joe was having a fist fight with a woman dressed as a Dark Angel. She was bopping him repetitively on the nose so he turned and fled, howling like a girl.

"That reminds me." Nora said and waited for Seymour to catch up. "Do you have any jobs for White-Lightning Joe at the theatre?"

"What are his qualifications?"

"Stealing." Nora said.

Seymour arched an eyebrow.

"He was going through a tough time and needed some money. He's reformed." She said.

Humphrey bit back a smile.

"Well, I do need a general dogsbody." Seymour nodded.

"I'll get him to come to the theatre and you can see what you think of him." Nora said.

"Alright. Tell him to pop by one morning at ten." Seymour said.

"Thanks, Seymour." Nora appreciated.

He grinned.

They reach the entrance to the start of The Ghost Trail or Ghost Hunt as it was sometimes called. It was located down a winding, cobbled alleyway between a shop called 'Into the Blue' which sold expensive blue and white porcelain and ornaments, and an antique shop called 'Solid Memories', near The Duke's Pie and Albert's print shop. It backed onto the town hall. The old town jail and dungeons had been built in the mid-19th century and was visited by ghost seekers from all around the country. It also hosted comedy acts, theatre groups, bands and dances.

At the end of the alleyway was a tall, gothic iron cell gate. Next to it was a ticket booth where a man in costume sat.

"Evening!" He called cheerfully.

"This is spooky." Nora whispered to Heather.

Heather agreed.

"Hello. We have a table booked for six in the dungeon but first we would like to go on the Ghost Trail."

"Of course. That'll be twelve pounds, please."

"Is it only two pounds each?"

"Yes." The ghostly figure nodded, printing some tickets.

"That's a bargain."

"It's a Shriek-Week special." He said. "Do any of you have a heart condition?"

They looked at one another.

"Er...no."

"Pacemakers or epilepsy?"

They shook their heads.

"Just to warn you, there will be some strobe lighting and some frights." The ticket man said.

"Cool." Milton enthused.

Once they had paid, Cara took the tickets and handed them around.

"WELCOME!" A voice like whip crack then exclaimed.

Cara and Heather grabbed onto one another with a scream. They looked towards the cell gate. A man dressed as a Victorian jailer stood there, grinning.

"May I have your tickets, please?" A woman beside him asked.

They all passed their tickets to the woman who made a little tear in each before handing them back. She then disappeared into the shadows.

"Ah, so what do we have here?" The jailer then asked, suddenly transforming into character. "The sorriest lot of prisoners I ever saw. You've all been sentenced to time in the Castletown Jailhouse, and you'll be wishing you hadn't been born by the time your stint is over."

With a clanking and clunking he used his keys to unlock the cell door.

"Follow me then, come on! Move along there!" He said and the group passed though the cell doors and into the lobby. They entered a small, cramped stone room. It was almost pitch black with a solitary candle flickering to the side.

A man in a hooded robe emerged.

"I am The Master." He said and slammed the door behind them. It was so dark and claustrophobic that Nora clutched onto Humphrey. They listened with bated breath as the Master locked them in. Shadows danced about eerily as the solitary candle flickered.

Their host then began to tell them stories about all the gruesome and terrifying characters who been convicted in the court rooms upstairs and then imprisoned in the cells and jailhouse and who now haunted the rooms and halls.

All scepticism as to the reality of ghosts left the group as they entered into the world of Castletown spectres and convicts. There were moments of sheer fright and it felt as though none of them would ever emerge.

The Master took the group through tight, stone corridors into ancient prison cells. There were terrifying waxworks standing in the corners of cells, scary sounds, and groans, rattling of chains and strobe lighting as well as gruesome props, people who looked like waxworks but then suddenly moved with knives or axes raised, and blasts of dry ice. Nora decided that if she didn't have a heart condition before going in then she would have one now.

The ghost tour took half an hour but it felt like a lifetime. When it was finally over and they entered the bright lobby in front of the dungeon, they all breathed a sigh of relief, praised The Master and decided that was the most frightening experience ever.

"I'm not going to be able to sleep knowing all that took place just across the road from me." Nora said, sipping a glass of lemonade with a trembling hand.

Humphrey chuckled.

"I have to admit I was genuinely scared in there."

"They should make it eighteen rated." Heather said, fanning herself with her torn ticket.

"That was awesome!" Milton gushed, although he admitted that he too was terrified at some points.

"A good actor." Seymour praised. "Although, it's not as scary as The Woman in Black play."

"Oh great." Nora grimaced.

While they waited for their table in the dungeons they read some information about the foyer. As well as historical facts about the jailhouse, prison cells and dungeons there was a history of Halloween parties. Nora read that they had been taking place for thousands of years, with people enjoying Halloween celebrations in Cole before the time of the Romans.

The ancient Celts used to place skeletons in doorways to represent their dead ancestors and the Irish invented the Jack O'Lantern, although they used all manner of vegetables to symbolise the heads of the dead.

Carving pumpkins came from North America. There the tradition of wearing spooky costumes, trick or treating and other activities developed into what Halloween celebrations are today.

A robed monk arrived to show them to their table.

The dungeon was eerie and atmospheric but decorated brilliantly. The lighting glowed orange from myriads of candles in the heads of carved pumpkins, as well as stringed lights and real flames dancing in wall sconces. The windows were barred but there were two bold fire exits so it didn't feel as terrifying as the journey through the Victorian prison cells. A long buffet table against one whole wall contained the food for the evening and numerous round tables with chairs were located throughout the room.

Other people were arriving. Nora noticed several regulars from The Secondhand Bookworm, including

Spencer, his wife and their friend, Mal. When he noticed the bookshop group, Spencer led his friend over.

"Evening. Here for the horror stories?" He asked with a smirk.

"We just went on the Ghost Trail." Cara told him.

"Terrifying isn't it." Spencer said eagerly. "This is my friend Mal."

"Hello." Mal said.

He was as tall as Spencer with white skin and dark round eyes in hollow sockets. He had shoulder length grey hair and wore a suit.

"Hello." Everyone chorused.

"We'll be coming into the bookshop on Friday." Spencer assured.

"I'm looking forward to exploring your occult section." Mal said softly.

Nora smiled politely.

"Enjoy the show and the food." Spencer said and they left.

"He reminded me of Professor Snape." Heather whispered.

Seymour laughed.

They sat and enjoyed bottomless Prosecco and then listened to ghostly tales from the stage for an hour. The stories were mesmerising and unnerving. In the queue for the buffet they reminisced over the macabre narratives until Nora was almost put off eating. After they had devoured their meal there was an enactment of a hideous and gruesome era from Castletown's history which included beheadings, hauntings, plagues, witch hunts and hangings until Nora decided she wasn't going to get any sleep that night.

Everything finally finished close to midnight.

They left the dungeons through the alleyway and emerged into the dark street.

"Well, that was petrifying." Cara admitted, hugging herself nervously.

"Very chilling." Humphrey agreed.

"Can Milton and I stay over tonight, Nora?" Heather asked, hopefully. "I don't fancy driving back through the woods to Little Cove in the dark."

"Yes please!" Nora appreciated gratefully.

"Thanks, sis." Milton grinned, giving her a hug.

"We can all sleep in the lounge." Nora decided, thinking of her wardrobe.

Humphrey grinned, pleased that Nora wouldn't be alone.

They said their goodbyes, laughed about being so scared, Nora and Humphrey kissed goodbye and after gathering by the front door to Nora's flat, Nora, Milton and Heather waved Cara, Seymour and Humphrey off. Once she was inside with her siblings, Nora closed her front door and locked it up securely, trying not to think of jailhouse ghosts and witches as she fled up her stairs after her screaming brother and sister.

7 THE HOUSE OF COFFINS

"Do you sell tea towels because I collect them in every town I go to?"

Nora looked up from the till where she was gathering a variety of note and coin denominations for the calls day.

A large lady wearing what was obviously a wig was staring expectantly at Cara who was seated beside Nora behind the counter.

"No. We just sell books." Cara replied, hiding the half eaten cookie that was her breakfast.

"Oh." The woman sulked.

"Have you looked in 'Bits and Bobs' down Market Street?" Betty asked helpfully. "They do some lovely items in there and I expect there are some beautiful tea towels with images of Castletown on them."

"Thanks. I'll take a look. Where did you say?"

Betty led the lady over to the window and pointed.

"Just down that street there."

"Don't touch me." The woman said, moving her arm from where it was pressed against Betty's.

Betty jumped.

"Oh, I'm terribly sorry." She apologised and as the woman left she gave Nora and Cara a look.

Cara almost choked on her cookie.

"I think you're going to have one of *those* days." Nora chuckled.

"Dratted old bag." Betty muttered, glaring after the woman. "Oh. Now that's justice. She almost got run over by Georgina."

Nora looked up to see The Secondhand Bookworm van reversing into a space outside the delicatessen. The woman in the wig had had to stumble back onto the kerb to avoid being propelled backwards by the front bumper of the van. Betty cackled with glee.

Georgina emerged from the driver's seat and stared at the woman in the wig who was obviously giving her a mouthful. Ignoring her, Georgina clip-clopped over to The Secondhand Bookworm.

"Morning, ladies!" She greeted cheerfully.

"Oh, Georgina. You should have run that woman over." Betty lamented.

"What?" Georgina asked, removing her sunglasses.

"Some woman was rude to Betty." Cara said, finishing off her cookie.

"You almost squashed her with the van." Nora said.

"Oh *her*. I had no idea what she was moaning about." Georgina said. "Silly lady should wait before she tries to cross the road."

"This is not a good start to the day." Nora mumbled to Cara who laughed.

"Ready to go, Nora?" Georgina asked, spreading a selection of new local guides by David Bone in a row on the counter.

"Yes. I have some money."

"Hopefully we'll spend it all." Georgina said, examining the decorations. "Very festal."

Cara smiled.

"Come along then." Georgina urged Nora.

Nora grabbed her bag and hurried around the counter.

"Have a lovely day." Betty said.

"Thank you, Betty." Georgina sang, Nora waved and they headed off out of the shop to the van.

"Uh-oh." Nora said.

"Uh-oh, what?" Georgina asked, slipping on her sunglasses.

"I spy White-Lightning Joe."

Georgina looked sharply in the direction Nora nodded, in time to see White-Lightning Joe's plump form dive into a watch shop near the corner of Market Street, having obviously noticed them.

"Ssssssss!" Georgina scowled, shaking her head. "Yes, he had *better* run from me."

Nora laughed.

They jumped into the van and Georgina passed Nora a black, zip up file which contained a sheet of information displaying times, names and addresses of their calls.

"Not many then." Nora read happily.

She slipped the purse of money inside and buckled on her seatbelt quickly.

"No, hopefully we won't be long." Georgina said, revving the van engine and startling an old lady. "I've put the first address into the Tom-Tom already."

Nora looked at the satnav stuck to the front window and then pitched back in her seat as Georgina sped off from her parking space, went up onto the curb as she turned the corner and was soon speeding over the bridge that led out of Castletown.

"Humphrey said you had a good evening at the dungeon." Georgina smiled, ignoring the Tom-Tom as a lady's voice demanded she do a U-turn.

"It was very scary."

"I'll have to go with Troy, Jane and her new man. We're looking for somewhere to go for a nice night out."

"You should." Nora agreed, thinking fondly of her former colleague Jane who had left to run a ballet school.

'Take the second exit.' The Tom-Tom said.

"No!" Georgina argued. "Stupid woman. I know how to get to Walltown and it's better my way."

Nora grinned, enjoying the view through the window.

The first call was at a farmhouse with a large barn next to it, both owned by a man named Mr Tostevin. The bookshop van bounced down a private drive to a gravelled opening in front of the house. Nora and Georgina both stared at a black funeral hearse parked outside as well as what looked like a coffin being used as a trough for flowers.

"Has someone died?" Nora asked, eyeing the hearse.

"I hope not! He made the appointment on Monday so he would have told me about a funeral, surely."

As Georgina parked and turned off the engine the front door of the farmhouse opened. A scruffy Yorkshire terrier bounded out followed by a tall man. The man wore a tunic with a belt, jeans and heavy boots and was carrying a hammer. He had a high forehead, sharp nose and wide set eyes.

Nora glanced nervously at the mallet.

"Hello. From the bookshop." Georgina greeted, ignoring the dog turning circles at her feet.

"Yes. I can see that on your van." Mr Tostevin read. Georgina smiled tightly.

"Yes, quite. I hope we're not interrupting anything?"

Nora bent down to stroke the little dog which began to give her quick warm licks and roll over to show its tummy.

"You're lovely. Hello, aw you're so sweet." Nora fussed.

"No, I said ten thirty." Mr Tostevin said.

"Yes." Georgina looked at the hearse.

"Oh, that's my car." Mr Tostevin explained. "I'm a coffin-maker."

Nora stared. Georgina stared. The Yorkie jumped up and ran off towards some flowers.

"Oh. My. What an interesting job."

"Yeah, it is. Some people feel uneasy about my occupation but there's a large demand now for handmade and natural coffins. I also make caskets."

"What's the difference?" Nora asked.

"A coffin has six sides. A casket is a four sided funeral box." Mr Tostevin explained.

Georgina gave Nora a look that warned her not to ask any more questions.

"We've come to look at your books." Georgina then hinted.

"Yes, I know that." Mr Tostevin said. "I keep them in the barn. This way."

Nora kept an eye on the hammer Mr Tostevin was carrying and they walked with him towards the large outhouse. He opened a door set in the side and gestured for them to go first. The Yorkie followed, yapping.

The space inside the barn was enormous. Georgina and Nora stepped inside and then stopped short, staring. The whole area was filled with coffins, some upright and leaning against the walls or beams, most on stands and some in the process of being made. It looked like a scene from Dracula. Nora paled.

"I keep a lot of things in the coffins I make before they are sold. Fleece coffins are becoming more popular in Britain these days." Mr Tostevin said easily, passing them and walking between the coffins.

"What?" Nora couldn't help asking.

"These here." He indicated with his hammer. "They're made from pure wool with a cardboard liner. Fully biodegradable. I also make willow coffins and bamboo coffins. It's surprising how many people do opt for burial rather than cremation but my coffins are suitable for both."

Georgina's expression was one of calm horror.

"There's a common fallacy that the head of a cremated body explodes if there isn't a hole in it, like a microwaved potato with no perforations. My brother works at the crematorium and has assured me this has never happened."

Nora thought she might scream and vomit at the same time.

Georgina cleared her throat.

"We're here to look at your books, not shop for coffins." She said loudly.

"This way." Mr Tostevin said mildly. "These coffins I made for me and my relatives so I keep my books in them until the coffins are needed."

Nora followed Georgina tentatively through the maze of sarcophagi, grimacing. They reached a row of lovely crafted coffins and Mr Tostevin began to lift up the lids to reveal rows and rows of books. The Yorkie danced about at their feet.

"I do have a library in the house but these are excess books I've not read in a long time." Mr Tostevin said and stood waiting while still holding his hammer.

"Okay." Georgina said, warily. "Well we'll have a look through and see which ones we can use."

She looked at Nora who didn't know whether to laugh or cry at the pair of them rummaging through books in a row of coffins. Nora started with the one nearest to her. While she browsed through the rows, her mind became absorbed in literature as she plucked out various interesting tomes. They were of a variety of subjects. She then gasped.

"What?" Georgina whispered.

"Is it? Could it be?" She opened a green cloth book titled 'Carry on, Jeeves', written by P G Wodehouse. She checked the date. "1925. A first edition!" She whispered back to Georgina. "Oh, please can I put this by for the Duke?"

Georgina's lips twitched.

"Still have a crush on him, have we?"

"Yes." Nora admitted. "Of course I do. But it's not ever going to come to anything so I bask in my fondness for our new local Duke."

Georgina snorted.

"It doesn't have a wrapper but the first one didn't." Nora mused, pondering the black image of a man kneeling down before a butler on the front board beneath the title and author name.

"One for the 'yes' pile." Georgina nodded.

They made their way through the coffins and ended up with several armfuls.

"I can offer you fifty pounds for these." Georgina told Mr Tostevin. You have a first edition of a P G Wodehouse here so that has bumped up the price."

"I accept your offer." He nodded.

"Would you like cash or a cheque?"

"Cash will do nicely."

They paid him and he helped carry some of the books to the van. Nora unlocked the side door, constructed three collapsible blue boxes and arranged the books neatly inside while Georgina spoke with Mr Tostevin. Nora was sure she heard her assuring him she was not interested in being measured for her coffin.

Mr Tostevin picked up the Yorkie as Georgina reversed, Nora gave a polite wave and at last they were hurtling back down the drive.

"Well I can't say that wasn't fitting for Shriek-Week." Nora said, wiping her hands on some wet wipes.

"Quite!" Georgina shook her head. "Whatever next! I have to tell Troy about that."

She pressed autodial on the van phone and the next moment the sound of ringing filled the cab. Nora was trying to hold steady as she typed the next address into the Tom-Tom but Georgina was driving like a Formula 1 racer so it was a battle.

"Hiya!" Troy's voice finally answered.

"Hello, love. You wouldn't believe where Nora and I have just been." Georgina said.

"Where have you been?" Troy asked with his strong American accent.

"To a barn filled with coffins. All the books were in the coffins."

Troy laughed.

"You gotta be joking me."

"No. I wish I was." Georgina said.

"For real?"

"Yes. For real." Georgina insisted and grinned at Nora.

They chatted for a while until Troy said: 'I gotta split' and after lots of declarations of affection that made Nora feel queasy, they hung up.

The second call that day was further out in the wilds near Walltown in a little village. They pulled up before a cemetery and stared out the window.

"Edward Powe. He's a Baptist vicar." Nora read.

"Ah yes. Nice chap. He has a library of theology books."

They climbed out the van and stood looking for the vicarage. It seemed to be located the other side of the cemetery and the only access to it was through a short wooden gate and along a winding pathway amidst crypts, tombs, mausoleums and graves.

The wind had picked up and the sky was overcast. The village seemed empty.

"This feels like an episode from Doctor Who." Nora said as they opened the gate and began through the cemetery.

Georgina agreed.

"Look at all these Elizabeths!" Nora exclaimed when they were a quarter of the way through.

They both stared at all the tombstones surrounding them. Each one belonged to an Elizabeth, covering at least one hundred and fifty years.

"That's weird." Georgina said.

They continued on.

Nora yelped when a black cat ran across her path hissing. She almost tripped, turned to steady herself and screamed. Facing her was a stone effigy exactly like a Weeping Angel from Doctor Who.

Georgina laughed.

"I daren't move." Nora gasped, holding stock still.

"Don't be daft." Georgina shook her head.

Tentatively Nora continued on. She looked back over her shoulder at the Weeping Angel and was sure it had moved closer to her. Georgina jumped when Nora ran past her.

"Honestly, Nora!" Georgina laughed.

They finally reached the vicarage which was a rambling old house with a carved pumpkin sitting on the doorstep. They rang the bell and were greeted by Reverend Powe.

"Ah, come in ladies." He smiled, stepping back. "Thank you for coming. The books are this way."

"Thank you." Georgina smiled.

Nora kept close, following the vicar and Georgina down a hallway and into a study.

"I'd like you to take a look at all the books in these cases." Vicar Powe indicated.

"Ah, alright. Now what's the story with these?" Georgina asked.

"I've collected them over the years to assist with my ministry, now I need to cull. I suffer from avarice."

"Okay, we'll see what we can help you with." Georgina smiled.

The vicar seated himself behind his desk and began to cut out a chain of paper people. Nora stared at him until Georgina nudged her.

"Pull out anything you think will sell." She said.

Nora nodded and began to scan the shelves.

There was a whole shelf of Biblical and scriptural colouring books. Nora was distracted by these for a while until Georgina pointedly cleared her throat.

"Alright Revered Powe, we're done-did." Georgina said five minutes later. "I'm afraid I can't really help you with these. They're not books that will sell to my customers."

"What can I do with them?" The vicar asked cheerfully.

"You could donate them." Georgina suggested.

"I could have a parish bazaar and have a book stall I suppose. Sorry you had a wasted trip."

"It's no problem." Georgina assured.

The vicar led them to the front door.

"Thank you for coming."

"You're welcome." Georgina called without looking back and they walked through the cemetery once more.

Nora thought she saw an ecto-mist between two large overgrown mausoleums. A crow landed on a cross. Many of the tombs were chipped and an eerie atmosphere hung over the whole cemetery. When they finally reached the van, Nora looked back at the

Weeping Angel, noticing that there were several more. She dived into the van with a yelp.

"I think we should pay a visit to the Pumpkin Shop on our way to the next call." Georgina decided once they were on their way again.

"Ooooh!" Nora agreed.

"It's near Seatown, in the countryside. A lovely farm shop that is famous for fruit murals. The barns next to the shop are all festooned with carved pumpkins and squashes." Georgina explained.

"I can pick up a few to carve." Nora nodded.

"Off we go then!" Georgina said and put her foot down.

The Pumpkin Shop glowed orange in the distance as The Secondhand Bookworm van approached it. In the fields surrounding it and encompassing the three barns were scarecrows, decorated for Halloween. Crows soared about the sky and had settled in droves on the roofs of the shop and barns, squawking and crowing loudly.

Nora and Georgina felt like children as they scrambled out of the van in excitement. There were lots of people admiring the displays and picking out different sized pumpkins. Nora and Georgina visited the pumpkin mosaic which was behind a row of long tables where varieties of pumpkins, gourds and squashes were for sale. The mosaic was a colourful picture made out of green, black, orange and red pumpkins and squashes to portray a large carriage pulled by mice.

It had been created using about two thousand pumpkins supported by small stakes, on boards leaning slightly back and filled with straw. The people who created it ran Castletown Festival which took place every summer.

On the tables was an unusual selection of many varieties of pumpkins and squashes, all different shapes and sizes and from all over the world. As well as whole pumpkins ready for carving there were pumpkins that had already been carved. The shapes in them were diverse such as black cats, spiders, faces and stars.

Nora snapped some photos for Instagram and then chose a large orange pumpkin to carve and place on the doorstep to her flat, as well as some squashes to cook. Georgina bought six large pumpkins and some squashes. There were also ceramic pumpkins for tea lights so Nora bought one of those.

They popped into the shop and ordered some pumpkin soup served with great chunks of bread and cheese and sat inside to eat. The soup was thick and creamy and made from the blue-grey Crown Prince squash.

"I'm looking forward to carving this." Nora said as they popped their crates of pumpkins and squashes into the back of the van among the books and flat packed boxes.

"Troy loves Halloween. He asked for lots of pumpkins to carve for the weekend." Georgina said.

"Are you both going trick or treating?" Nora teased.

"You may jest but he actually suggested that."

Nora laughed.

"Well, I'll make sure I have some candy put aside for when you call." She said.

Georgina laughed, they jumped into the cab and set off for their next call, well satiated and topped up with Cucurbita.

8 APOCALYPTIC ZOMBIE WALK

The Secondhand Bookworm van chugged merrily along the A27 to the third house call of that day. According to the satnav the house was located on the Park Town road, with the need to take a sharp left so as to enter the drive. When they reached it, Georgina slammed on the brakes and whipped into the driveway amidst beeping and fist waving from the other drivers behind.

"Sorry." Georgina sang.

Nora pitched forward in her seat as they stopped before a tall black front door.

"What a gloomy old house." She observed.

It looked like something out of a ghost film with lofty dark windows in endless bays, pointed roofs and white plasterwork that had darkened with age, was cracked in places and missing huge chunks. There were no flowers or garden ornaments in sight.

They climbed out of the van, Nora grabbed the calls file and knocked on the front door. Several minutes passed without any reply.

"Drat. I hope he hasn't forgotten." Georgina said. "I'll give him a call. What's his name and number?"

Nora opened the calls file and read them out to Georgina. She dialled the number into the shop mobile and stood waiting for Mr Muller to answer.

"Hello? Hello!" Georgina shouted into the phone. "Mr Muller? Miss Pickering from the bookshop. We're at your front door! Oh, okay. Thank you. Goodbye." She hung up. "He says he's a moment away."

They remained by the front door waiting and eventually a silver car turned into the driveway.

"Sorry." Mr Muller mumbled, stepping out.

He was a scruffy man in his late forties with a black baggy t-shirt that read 'blessing of the motorcycles', tie-dyed festival trousers and a check short tied around his waist. He had beaded bracelets on his wrists and a red neck cloth.

"No problem." Georgina said politely.

He unlocked the door and let them into a dark corridor.

"The books are in there." He said, pointing to a door on the left.

"Okay." Georgina said and she and Nora headed toward it as Mr Muller scurried into the kitchen.

"Odd." Nora whispered as Georgina opened the door.

They stepped inside and froze.

The room was lined with bookcases and tanks. The tanks were full of snakes. Occult objects decorated the free spaces on the walls, with black sofas draped in multi-coloured throws and a long coffee table filled with bits and bobs. The scent of hippy incense drifted into the room from the hall.

Mr Muller came in, brushed past them and lit two joss sticks.

"Don't mind the snakes." Mr Muller mumbled. "I'm looking after two for a friend. Two are mine."

"What types are they?" Georgina asked.

She and Nora moved to investigate.

"This is a royal python. These two are California Kingsnakes and this one is a Western Hognose."

Nora examined them with interest. They were magnificently patterned.

"Lovely." Georgina grimaced.

"My books are here." Mr Muller indicated quietly.

Georgina coughed because of the incense. Nora's eyes stung.

"Ah. Occult and witchcraft. Very apt for Halloween." Georgina observed. "What's the story with these then?"

"I simply need to have a clear out before I move." Mr Muller replied. "It's just my personal collection from the past twenty years."

"I'll pull out any I can use and make you an offer for them." Georgina said, scanning the shelves.

Mr Muller nodded.

He watched as Nora and Georgina made their way through his cases.

"Lots for Spencer I expect." Georgina said.

"Hmm." Nora screwed up her nose at all the horrible titles and subjects such as Wicca books of spells, hidden magic, occult truths, numerous tomes by Aleister Crowley, different editions of Harry Potter, books about runes, tarot cards and pentagrams, enneagrams, séances, witches, occult philosophy, the book of Enoch, vampire novels and a 'supernatural TV colouring book'.

By the time they had completed looking through two cases, Nora wanted a bath in holy water.

"Oh, these are nice." Georgina said.

At least four shelves held a collection of Edgar Allen Poe books, numerous editions and printings, some illustrated by artists such as Harry Clarke and W Heath Robinson.

"They can all go." Mr Muller said.

"We'll have all these." Georgina whispered to Nora, pleased.

Eventually there was a large pile of books on the floor. Georgina knelt down and whispered prices to herself.

"Right, all done-did." She finally announced, standing up. "I can offer you two hundred and ten pounds for these."

Mr Muller nodded.

"Thanks." He mumbled.

"Would you like a cheque or cash?"

"Cash please."

"Of course. Do we have enough, Nora?"

Nora nodded, reaching for the purse.

"Yes, I expect so." She said, trying not to choke on the incense surrounding them.

"Here, I'll count it out and you go to the van and collect all the boxes." Georgina offered.

Nora passed her the calls file and fled the house, taking gulps of fresh air once she was outside.

"I'm going to smell like a hippy all day." She grumbled to herself, unlocked the van and began to pull out flat packed boxes.

It took a good quarter of an hour to load up all the books and carry them out to the van. Mr Muller just stood watching them, making Nora feel uneasy. Once the van was full up and the boxes arranged, with the crates of pumpkins, squashes and gourds that had purchased placed carefully to the side, they bid Mr Muller goodbye, jumped into the van and set off.

"I'm not very happy with all those evil books behind me." Nora said, wiping her hands with wet wipes. "And I smell like the Drunk-Boy."

"The Drunk-Boy?" Georgina asked.

"One of our regulars. You know, he spends loads of money on art books while he is drunk or high on magic mushrooms. He smells of Nag Champa."

"Oh dear." Georgina laughed. "Well let's hope the next call has a selection of lovely books on flowers and cooking and bunnies and sunshine."

"I doubt it." Nora sighed and set about typing the next address into the Tom-Tom.

The next call was located in Walltown. The bookshop van sped through the countryside into the ancient walled town and passed a woman walking a little scruffy dog.

"I don't want to go for a walk." Georgina said in a gruff voice, doing an impression of the dog.

Nora giggled.

The van phone began to ring so Nora pressed answer.

"Hello?" She greeted.

"Haaaaallllooooooooo." Cara's voice filled the cab.

"Hey!" Nora grinned.

"Hello." Georgina sang. "How's it going in Castletown?"

"Quite busy actually. We sold a load of books to a trade customer and lots of people are in the town today. We're on…four hundred and ten."

"Excellent!" Georgina said, pleased.

"Mr Hill wants to know if he can sell his books." Cara then said.

Georgina groaned.

"Wonderful."

"He want to bring them in tomorrow to Seatown. He asked for you."

"Well I have a hair appointment in Seatown at eleven. I can pop in and look at his books then."

"I'll let him know. Gotta go, there's a customer."

"Have a good day." Georgina said.

"See you later." Nora bade.

"Byeeeeee." Cara sang and they hung up.

The bookshop van soon arrived at the destination in Walltown. It was a pleasant block of flats not far from Walltown Park where fallow deer roamed gardens designed by Capability Brown.

Mrs Lewis buzzed them in and they knocked on the door of number 21a. The door opened to reveal a plump, wistful looking woman with long grey hair wearing a long purple and embroidered kaftan.

"From the bookshop." She said knowingly. "Please come in."

Georgina and Nora entered the flat and Mrs Lewis closed the door behind them.

"You both smell nice." She said.

"Oh. Our previous call had a lot of incense burning."

"Lovely." Mrs Lewis admired.

Nora noticed that the walls were hung with colourful paintings of hands, the Zodiac, a man's face with a third eye and modern paintings of the cosmos. She glanced at Georgina who smiled tightly.

"This way please. Now, let's start off with a glass of wine. Rose alright for you?" Mrs Lewis asked.

"Er..." Nora stared.

"I'm afraid I'm driving." Georgina pointed out.

"Not a small tipple?"

"No thank you." Georgina said and gave Nora a look.

"No thanks." Nora refused, biting back a smirk.

"I hope you don't mind if I do. I'm having a tough day today." She led them into a lounge where a drinks cabinet was located next to a bookcase. A selection of books had been piled neatly onto a white coffee table.

"Are these your books?" Georgina asked.

"Yes. Those are for sale."

Nora and Georgina bent over them while Mrs Lewis filled a large glass with sloshes of pink wine.

"I'm an online clairvoyant." She said.

"Oh. How does that work?" Georgina asked.

"People correspond with me for psychic advice. Usually by email. But I do chats as well. And tarot readings by email. Can I read your palms."

"No thank you." Georgina said.

Nora shoved her hands in the pockets of her jeans.

"You have a strong aura." Mrs Lewis told Nora.

"I'm afraid I can't help you with any of these." Georgina told Mrs Lewis.

Mrs Lewis's face fell.

"None of them?"

"No. Sorry."

She burst into tears.

"Oh, I knew because of my horoscope that today would be a bad day!" She bawled.

Nora stared.

"I'm sorry." Georgina said tightly. "We just visited a house with a whole library of occult books and I purchased a lot about tarot cards and astrology."

Mrs Lewis dabbed her eyes on a hanky, blew her nose loudly and gulped down her wine.

"Very well. Let us hope my fortunes turn tomorrow. Here's my card if you ever require readings."

Nora and Georgina couldn't leave quick enough.

Mrs Lewis saw them to the door and sniffed as they walked hurriedly away.

"For a psychic she didn't see that coming." Georgina said.

Nora smothered a laugh.

"Thank goodness we only have one call left." Georgina said and once they were in the van she put her foot down and they sped from Walltown, leaving Mrs Lewis watching them from her window, sobbing.

The last call of the day was only five minutes outside Castletown in a large country house. Mr Flood was a lifelong bachelor who told them that he spent his days pottering about his estate enjoying the bliss of not having a nagging wife.

"I saw your advert in the paper and thought I should have a sort out of my books before I die. I don't have any relatives. My only sibling was a brother who was a Catholic priest." He explained, leading them down a long hallway.

"Oh I am sure you are a long way from personal judgment." Georgina smiled.

He chuckled.

"Well, one can never be too prepared. I don't want to leave a heap of earthly good for some poor souls to have to dispose of. I want all my excess possessions to gradually go." He said and led them into a large, spacious study.

"How freeing." Georgina approved.

"I have several cases on mythology and world history. I was a professor in Oxford for forty years."

"How wonderful!" Georgina admired.

"Please, have a look through and see if there is anything useful to you and your customers. I have no use for it all now."

"We'll look through and see what we can use." Georgina smiled.

"Would you like tea, or coffee?" He offered.

"No thank you, we just drank." Georgina refused and began to scan the shelves.

Nora was distracted by the arrival of a Westie called Tolkien. She sat and fussed over him until Georgina cleared her throat for the umpteenth time and Nora reluctantly went back to picking out saleable books.

Tolkien jumped and skipped about the room and Mr Flood played catch with him until Nora and Georgina were finished.

"I can use these, Mr Flood and they would be worth one hundred pounds to me. The rest of your collection is a little too specialist for my stock."

"Of course, I understand. Yes, that would be acceptable. Thank you." He nodded. "Now. Would you like these?"

He led them to six boxes stacked by the window.

"My brother Enda, the priest, fancied himself a bit of a writer." Mr Flood explained. "He wrote six detective novels in the fifties and had them privately printed by Chasuble Press, fifty copies of each. They're like G K Chesterton's Father Brown stories. No one was interested so he passed them on to me and they've sat in the guest bedroom for fifty years. Father Enda died five years ago."

Georgina shook her head.

"I'm sorry but they wouldn't be for me." She said.

Nora bounced from foot to foot.

"May I have a look?" She asked.

"Of course, my dear." Mr Flood nodded.

Georgina looked bemused.

They opened the flaps of the first box. Nora picked out a copy. It was the usual length of a standard paperback, beautifully presented and was book five in 'The Father Ulysses E. Flood Mysteries', about a Catholic priest turned sleuth.

"Oh, they're wonderful." Nora gushed. "The Body in the Priest Hole. Book One." She read. The books were hardback editions and had been illustrated throughout with stunning black and white woodcuts.

"You are welcome to have them all, young lady." Mr Flood offered.

"Oh! May I?" Nora looked at Georgina.

"If you want." She laughed. "I'm sure we can squeeze them in the van."

"Thank you!" Nora appreciated, regarding her new acquisition with delight.

"Here." Mr Flood walked over to his desk. "You can have the copyright to them as well. If you write down your name and address I'll have my solicitor organise that. Then you can have them published in a modern edition if you ever feel inspired."

"Wow. Thank you." Nora breathed, thrilled.

Nora gave Mr Flood her details, they paid, loaded up the van with his books and managed to fit in the six boxes of Father Enda Flood's books in the back by the doors, bade Tolkien and Mr Flood goodbye and set off.

"What are you going to do with all of those books?" Georgina asked Nora.

"I was thinking about starting a book club." Nora said. "We had some werewolves in yesterday who were members of a Jane Austen book club."

Georgina nearly choked on her water.

"And I've often thought about a joining or starting a book club, but not the usual kind, I would want to do something special and eccentric. This series is perfect! We could read one a week."

"You're welcome to use The Secondhand Bookworm after hours." Georgina offered.

"Oh, really?! That's so kind. Thank you."

"You're welcome." Georgina grinned. "Now let's head to Castletown and get unloading. We'll start with yours first."

Nora smiled happily and they set off.

Back in Castletown, Nora and Georgina piled up the 'Father Ulysses E. Flood Mysteries' boxes at the bottom of Nora's staircase in her flat and then drove the short distance down the hill to The Secondhand Bookworm.

Georgina managed to find a place a few shops away from the bookshop and reversed into it so fast that Nora squealed. Georgina turned off the engine.

"We'll lock up the van and then you and Cara can unload once we've had a cup of tea." She said.

"Okay!" Nora nodded, unclipping her belt.

She noticed numerous zombies milling around the town so checked her watch, recalling that the zombie handing out leaflets for the zombie walks taking place on Thursday and Saturday had told them it began at four o'clock. There was half an hour to go.

Inside The Secondhand Bookworm, Cara was busy working on the computer. Betty was nowhere to be seen.

"Hi!" Cara greeted, pleased.

"We're worn out." Georgina replied.

"Shall I make some tea?"

"You read our minds."

Cara jumped up, grinned at Nora and headed off for the kitchen.

"BETTY!" Georgina called up the stairs.

"Oh! Hello, Georgina." Betty's muffled voice sailed down. There was the creaking of the floor and Betty made her way to the top of the stairs.

"We're here for tea." Georgina said.

"Oh lovely, Georgina." Betty smiled.

Betty was in her mid-seventies. She worked part-time at The Secondhand Bookworm and was outrageous, with a sharp wit and dry sense of humour. She was also very sensitive about her age.

"I'll just finish off sorting this box of tuba music and then I'll be down." Betty said and blew Nora a kiss.

Nora waved and she and Georgina headed back to the front room.

Cara came back in.

"There's a letter here addressed to Mr. T. S. Bookworm." She said, digging out the post file.

Georgina arched an eyebrow. Nora laughed.

"Mr The Secondhand Bookworm?" She snorted.

"Yes." Cara giggled.

Georgina took it.

"Oh dear." She sighed, sitting down on the stool. "Here." She passed Nora the van key. "While the kettle's boiling why don't you two bring in a couple of boxes of books to start marking up?"

"Okay." Nora and Cara said in unison.

Georgina opened her letter and scoffed.

"It's just an invitation to the Silent Halloween Disco Boat that will be mooring on the river Saturday night." She said.

"Whaaaaaaat?!" Cara exclaimed.

"That sounds amazing." Nora said.

"Well you can read about it when you come back with some boxes. Off you go." Georgina said bossily.

Cara and Nora left hastily, grinning.

"I like the sound of the silent Halloween disco boat." Cara told Nora.

"Why would it be silent?" Nora mused.

"Oh, you have headphones linked to the music so you can dance and enjoy it without being a nuisance to the neighbourhood. Seymour and I went to a silent disco in Seatown. It was funny when we took off our headphones to speak to one another and all we could hear was shuffling and some people singing along out of tune."

Nora laughed.

"It sounds bizarre."

Cara agreed.

They grabbed two boxes each after Nora had rummaged for the first edition 'Carry on, Jeeves'. When they returned to the shop Betty was down from upstairs and had finished making the tea and Georgina had popped into the yard to inspect the new air conditioning unit attached to the estate agent wall.

"Ah, tea." Nora appreciated, picking a mug.

"No sugar in any of them." Betty smiled.

"Aren't we all good?" Cara pointed out, taking a sip of hers.

"The cheek of the estate agents putting that monstrous object up in my yard." Georgina glowered, texting Troy about it. "I'll pop round there in a bit and see what we can do about it."

"Hmm. It is loud and intrusive." Nora nodded.

"Perhaps get some more boxes in." Georgina then decided, ending a text and then reading emails on the computer monitor. "I'd like the van unloaded and there's no time like the present."

"Okay." Nora nodded.

"Enjoy your tea first." Georgina said.

"Thanks." Nora took a sip.

"I'm so excited to be working with you tomorrow, Nora." Betty smiled.

"We always have an interesting day." Nora chuckled.

"As long as there aren't too many greyheads." Betty then glowered.

Nora laughed.

"Oh, Georgina. How much on the First Edition 'Carry on, Jeeves'?" Nora asked, walking over to the box she had carefully placed it in.

"I'll look it up and price it for you." Georgina said with a small smirk.

Nora passed it to her, smiling back at Betty and Cara's knowing grins.

They drank their tea and then Nora and Cara headed back for the van while Betty started marking up the books. A large mass of people had gathered at the top of the hill. As Nora and Cara rummaged in the back of the van and dragged two boxes each towards them, and immense sound of groaning, moaning, screeching and screaming came from the top of the hill.

The apocalyptic zombie walk had started down the hill and was heading towards them.

"Oh my." Cara stared.

Nora's mouth dropped open.

It was actually a terrifying sight. At least a hundred zombies were slouching, walking or staggering down the hill. They had taken over the whole road and all the pavements. People were taking photos, standing aside or diving into shops for a safer view. Several cars had to stop. Nora didn't envy the people in them, surrounded by zombies.

"Quick!" Nora gasped.

She and Cara picked up their boxes, locked up the van and rushed back the shop as the chaotic sounds of screaming, groaning and screeching followed them. Betty had stuck her head out the door.

"I'd better get back inside or people will think I'm one of them." She said as Nora and Cara reached the doorway.

Nora laughed.

"What on *earth* is going on out there?" Georgina asked, looking up from the computer monitor, confused.

"The Zombie Walk." Cara said.

She dumped her boxes down quickly and dug out her iPhone.

"I have to film it!"

"They'll be a better view from the window upstairs." Nora said.

"Good idea!" Cara agreed.

Georgina shook her head as Nora and Cara hurried off to film the walk from the first floor window and take photos.

An old man with a checked shopper was hurrying as fast as he could in front of the zombies. He was ancient and shrivelled and kept looking back over his shoulder in fear. Nora recognised him as a local author who was

writing a book about the history of smuggling in
Castletown and had been plaguing the shop for months,
hoping Georgina would stock it once it was published.
He had popped in several times a week asking for advice
and giving them updates. His name was Mr Fink.

"Oh dear." Cara said, suppressing a smile.

They watched as he rushed along, finally wheeling
his shopper to the edge of the street a few shops away
from The Secondhand Bookworm, taking shelter with
several people as the zombies passed.

Some of the zombies turned on each other,
pretending to eat one another as they neared knots of
people watching them. There were a few people dressed
as soldiers with cap guns, pretending to fire on the
zombies as if attempting to contain them.

As they reached the square they began to gather,
groaning, moaning and raising their arms in typical
zombie fashion. The Michael Jackson song 'Thriller'
began to play and the zombies started to dance and sing
along to it.

Nora and Cara continued to take photos, leaning out
of the window and watching in amazement. Some of the
zombie dancing was in imitation of the zombies dancing
in the 'Thriller' video.

When the song finally finished there was a round of
applause and cheers from all the onlookers. Gradually
the zombies came out of character, chatted in the square
and headed off for pubs and parties or to visit the
Waxwork Tent. Nora and Cara looked at one another
and grinned. It had been a very interesting, slightly
frightening, but extremely entertaining Zombie
Apocalypse!

9 THE HALLOWEEN BALL

When Nora returned to the front room after the zombie attack, Georgina passed her the copy of 'Carry on, Jeeves'.

"Sixty five pounds." Georgina said.

"Great. Thanks." Nora smiled, wrote her name on a piece of paper, added the paper and book to a clear plastic bag and tucked it under the counter with the other reserved books.

"Did you enjoy that spectacle?" Georgina asked them with a smirk.

"It was amazing."

"There's another one on Saturday." Georgina said.

"Shall I dress as a zombie?" Nora teased.

Georgina gave her a look.

Nora and Cara joined Betty by the window to price the books from the calls. Just as Nora sat down on a small footstool, Mr Fink appeared, looking harassed after being chased by hundreds of zombies.

"Ah. Georgina! Just the person." He said, clicking his fingers.

Georgina smiled tightly.

"Hello, Mr Fink."

They all watched as he stepped down into the shop followed by the clunk of his shopper and a couple of loud parps, and approached the counter.

"Ah, hello ladies!" He said, noticing Nora, Cara and Betty behind him by the window. His gaze lingered on Betty who gave him a warning look. "Hello again, old dear." He said, despite the glare.

Betty, who hated being called 'old', scowled.

Cara smothered a giggle behind a book she was marking up.

"Hello, Mr Fink." Nora replied, trying not to giggle, too.

"Now, Georgina. My book has finally been published and I have been sent several boxes but I have taken them all to the museum to sell. They've been so supportive after all." Mr Fink said, cheerfully.

There was a deadly silence. Georgina stared at him.

"I beg your pardon?"

"Yes, I know I said you could stock them, ah, it's wonderful being in such demand at my age, your older member of staff over there will understand," he glanced back and winked at Betty, unable to hear the tirade of swearwords Betty hissed in response, "but I decided to have them exclusively stocked at Castletown Museum. A lot of my research came from their archives, I use some of their photographs and they have been a wonderful support."

"*I* have been a support with the advice I've offered!" Georgina said defensively.

"Yes, you have Georgina. You helped me decide on the format, publisher and all that and I am immensely grateful. It is a wonderful looking book."

"Good luck to you then!" Georgina said tersely.

"Ah, thank you Georgina. Yes, I am sure it will sell well and make a lot of money for the museum."

Nora was sure she could hear Georgina growling.

"Right, I shall be off. I am heading there now. They would like me to give a talk about my book for Halloween on Saturday. They have done a big display about smuggling just for me! How wonderful. Good day to you all." He said, turned and set off.

They all watching him drag his shopper up the step and depart with a final parp.

Betty made a rude gesture with her hand to his retreating form. Georgina couldn't help but smirk.

"The cheek of him. Such a rude old blighter!" Betty snarled.

"That *was* rather rude of him." Nora agreed. "Both what he said to you, Betty, and the audacity of bugging us for months about stocking his book and then taking it elsewhere."

"I agree." Cara said. "Very rude."

"Well, when the museum gets fed up with his mountains of books cluttering up their place they can forget coming to me to sell them!" Georgina decided aloofly. "Time waster."

They all muttered uncharitable things until Betty decided to make a round of tea and suggested adding brandy to it.

"Perhaps not." Georgina laughed.

"Shame." Betty winked and headed off for the kitchen.

Cara and Nora started putting aside occult books that they thought might interest Spencer.

"I'm really not happy about feeding his devilish obsession." Nora said.

"I know. But they sell." Georgina said, clicking on the computer.

"As long as you don't expect me to sell my soul." Nora said.

Georgina gave her a look. Cara giggled into a copy of 'The Book of the Sacred Magic of Abramelin the Mage' and added it to the Spencer pile.

"Look at this!" Nora then exclaimed.

She held up a hardback book in the style of a Haynes car manual. The title read 'Zombie Survival Manual: The complete guide to surviving a zombie attack (Owners Apocalypse Manual).'

Cara burst out laughing.

"You have to put that in the window!" She said.

Georgina shook her head.

"*What would you do in the event of a zombie apocalypse? Would you know how to protect your family, forage for food and hold your own if confronted by the undead? Packed with vital information about how to prepare yourself (mentally and physically) and your surroundings for attack, the Zombie Survival Manual will also include advice on how to flourish in a post-apocalyptic world.*" Nora said, reading the blurb.

She began to flick through it before pricing it up and placing it in the window. As she did so, several zombies wandered over eating crisps and saw it. A moment later a zombie popped its head in through the open doorway.

"Hi! How much for the Zombie Survival Manual?" She asked with a grin.

"Six pounds fifty." Nora replied.

"I'll take it. Mind if I come in?"

"No problem." Georgina sighed, beginning to get fed up with Castletown already. She never did last long in The Secondhand Bookworm, Castletown. "I'll let you ladies deal with this. I'm going next door about the air conditioning unit in the yard."

"Okay." Nora smiled, wondering what was going to be the result with that!

Georgina walked past the zombie with her nose screwed up. Nora bit back a smile.

She sold a few other books to the zombie as well who was joined by her friends. Cara had dug out 'Zombie Survival Transport Manual: Post-apocalyptic vehicles (all variations)' Haynes manual too which the first zombie also snapped up.

The zombies lumbered off groaning and then laughing, pleased with their shopping trip.

Betty returned from the kitchen with more tea.

"I hope those zombies didn't eat Georgina." She said.

Cara giggled.

"No. Georgina has gone to the estate agents to complain about the new air conditioning unit." Nora explained.

A man stepped into the shop.

"Is this the only bookshop in Castletown?" The man asked.

"Why?" Betty replied.

"Because I might prefer the other one."

Betty stared.

"This is the only one." She said flatly.

"Oh." He said and walked away.

Betty shook her head.

Two witches arrived, carrying cauldrons.

"Hello!"

"Hello!" They both greeted. They then broke into dramatic cackles while waving pretend magic wands.

Nora recognised one of them as Sherrie, a saleswoman from 'Kiddies Boutique' which was located in the town. Nora looked around for Twinkle, a little sausage dog that had accompanied her over Christmas, but was disappointed there was no sign of him.

"Hello again!" Sherrie greeted Nora. "We're promoting 'Kiddies Boutique' this Halloween. We have a good selection of Halloween costumes for babies and children in stock. Such as this little cute t-shirt that reads

'I was small then I *gruesome.*' May we leave some discount flyers?"

"Oh. Yes, sure." Nora nodded.

"I'll have one." Cara said.

Sherrie took one out of her cauldron and gave it to Cara while her witch friend passed Nora a small pile.

"I'm Hocus." She said.

"And I'm Pocus!" Sherrie added.

Both witches cackled again, waving their wands.

Betty clapped her hands.

"Where's Twinkle?" Nora asked.

"Oh. He had a busy day yesterday dressed as a pumpkin as we did our rounds. He's currently sleeping it off." Sherrie smiled.

Nora pouted.

"Well, have a Happy Halloween!" Hocus said.

"Goodbye!" Pocus waved and they clip-clopped off back into the street.

"I heard Georgina mention her witch hunt again." Cara said, pondering the retreating forms of the witches. "To find the culprit who gave Paul Kempe our shop codes that enabled him to break in over the summer."

"Oh dear." Nora grimaced.

"He's refusing to name his source." Cara then added.

"Yes, I heard that. Humphrey and I are testifying at his trial in November." Nora said.

Paul Kempe had been a former employee of The Secondhand Bookworm, Piertown. The Secondhand Bookworm in Piertown had been Georgina's first bookshop which had long since closed. She had fired him when she had discovered he was selling her stock on eBay for his own profit. That summer he had been in the process of robbing The Secondhand Bookworm one night but had been caught by Nora and Humphrey returning after an Abba concert up at the Duke's park estate. There had been no evidence he had broken in so

Georgina was convinced someone who worked at The
Secondhand Bookworm had been bribed to give him the
alarm codes. She had been planning a witch hunt ever
since and was often found staring at her employees with
varying expressions of suspicion.

"Well, there's no better time than Halloween for a
witch hunt." Cara said cheerfully.

"Yes, but it won't be pleasant." Nora pointed out.

"No it won't." Betty agreed. "And I shall probably be
burned at the stake or drowned just for *looking* like an
ugly old witch."

Nora burst out laughing.

"You *don't* look like a witch." Nora reassured her.

"This morning a girl asked me where I got my mask."
Betty said, but then winked.

Nora tried not to giggle.

Georgina returned.

"Well. We came to an agreement. They offered to
pay me five hundred pounds a year rent for the air
conditioning unit to stick out into our yard. I accepted.
So you'll have to just endure the racket when it's on and
you need the yard door open."

"Oh, great." Nora sighed.

"Don't moan young lady. Part of the money will go
towards an extra Christmas bonus for you, Cara and
Roger." Georgina promised.

Nora smiled broadly.

"We were just wondering when you're going to
conduct your witch hunt." Cara then piped in.

"My what?" Georgina asked.

"Your witch hunt for the perpetrator that gave Paul
Kempe the alarm codes." Cara said.

"Oh *him*." Georgina snarled. She shook her head.
"No. I don't need to do that anymore. The horrible little
man confessed to camping out with extra strong

binoculars across the road from each of the shops and watching a member or staff punch in the code."

"How inventive." Nora admitted.

"Hmm." Georgina frowned.

Cara shrugged, pricing a copy of 'The Art of Eating through the Zombie Apocalypse: A Cookbook and Culinary Survival Guide', which she had decided would go in the window.

"Looks like I won't be burned at the stake after all." Betty said cheerfully.

Georgina, Nora and Cara laughed and they continued pricing up the books.

Half an hour before closing time, Georgina decided she had had enough of Castletown. They had had an assortment of typical customers:

"Have you seen my cousin?" One man had asked while purchasing two new Ordinance Survey maps. He was dressed as an escaped lunatic patient.

"I don't know your cousin." Georgina had pointed out.

"He's dressed as the headless huntsman."

Georgina had turned away and gone back to her emails.

"Do you sell books for the Kindle?" The next customer had asked her. She was wearing an Alice in Wonderland Dress, covered in blood spatter.

Georgina had stared.

"Kindle books are eBooks."

"Yes. Do you sell any?"

"No." Georgina had replied, tightly and shown her a cold shoulder.

"Have you seen the Neanderthal?" A man buying train books had next enquired. He wore a t-shirt that read 'Cereal Killer'.

"The what?" Georgina had asked, ignoring Nora and Cara snorting into their books.

"My brother. He looks like a Neanderthal."

"No one in a costume has come in." Georgina had assured.

"Oh, it's not a costume. It's how he always looks."

"I think I saw him go upstairs." Betty had offered helpfully, much to Nora and Cara's amusement.

Three people buying postcards had also fussed over purchasing stamps. While Georgina was patiently cutting single Worldwide Postcard stamps from the little books of four, one man had asked:

"Have any people ever washed up on shore?"

"Er...not that I'm aware of." Georgina had replied.

"Where can I buy jumping jacks?" The woman with him had asked.

"I don't know. From a jumping jacks shop?" Georgina had replied irritably.

"Do you need a cleaner?" The last man had asked.

"Why. Do you think my shop is dirty?" Georgina had asked, hostile.

"No. I'm just looking for a job."

"We do the cleaning ourselves." Georgina had scowled.

Even the arrival of the Gorey-ent express hadn't done much to make Georgina want to stay in The Secondhand Bookworm to the end of the day. Especially not when another fifty zombies disembarked the carriages to attend the zombie apocalypse party that was taking place in several pubs that evening.

"That's it. Time to go, Nora." Georgina announced, just as the telephone began to ring. She picked it up and passed it to Betty.

"Good afternoon, The Secondhand Bookworm." Betty greeted glamorously.

"Do you have a copy of The Crystal Egg?" The voice at the other end asked.

"Oh. Who wrote it?"

"You don't know?!" The caller scoffed.

Betty's lips pursed.

"I'm afraid I haven't had the delight of discovering The Crystal Egg." She told the caller. "But I will be happy to find out the author."

'*H G Wells*.' Georgina wrote on the message pad and pointed to it.

Betty read it but then jumped.

"The rude sod just hung up on me!" She said.

Georgina bit back a smile. With a furious expression Betty dialled 1572 and was pleased to learn the caller hadn't concealed his number. She pressed the button to call back and when he answered 'hello?' she hung up on him. Georgina burst out laughing.

"I think I shall be glad when I leave for the New Forest on Sunday." Georgina sang, gathering her bags.

"Oh, how lovely Georgina. Are you going camping?" Betty asked.

"Yes, for three days." Georgina nodded.

"That sounds nice." Nora smiled, slinging the strap of her bag over her shoulder. "But also spooky, sleeping by an enormous forest close to Halloween."

"Seymour and I went camping in the New Forest at the end of summer." Cara joined in, not looking up from browsing through a copy of 'Several Occult money rituals' that Georgina had bought from the man's house with all the snakes.

"Oh, how wonderful, Cara. Did you have a nice time?" Betty asked.

"No. A donkey stuck its head in the car window surrounded by flies. It was like a horror movie."

Nora doubled up laughing.

Shaking her head, Georgina took hold of Nora's arm and began to lead her away.

"Well done today ladies." Georgina said.

"Have a nice time at the Duke's Halloween Ball." Cara bade, smirking.

"Look forward to working with you tomorrow, Nora." Betty waved.

"Bye." Nora said, still laughing at Cara's donkey experience.

"Text me some photos!" Cara called after her sister-in-law.

"I will." Nora promised and left The Secondhand Bookworm with Georgina after a typically crazy bookworm afternoon!

The Secondhand Bookworm van pulled up outside Nora's family home in Little Cove, about ten minutes' drive from Castletown.

"Thanks, Georgina." Nora smiled, gathering her things.

"You're welcome. Thank you for today. Look forward to seeing you tonight!" Georgina grinned.

"You too!" Nora said, jumped out the van, waved goodbye and Georgina screeched away, beeping her horn merrily at a moped carrying Nora's sister, Heather.

Nora waited for Heather to drive up to the gate.

"Hello!" Heather grinned, pulling off her helmet.

"Hi! How's your last year at college going then?" Nora asked.

"Oh, pretty much the same as the previous two." Heather shrugged. "I hope you don't mind but I've been in your old room admiring your costume over the past few nights. I can't wait to see you in it!"

"You can help me get ready if you like?" Nora grinned.

"I'd love to!" Heather nodded and they set off up the garden path.

The Duke's Halloween Ball started at nine o'clock but first there was a five course meal in the Earl's Hall of the New Castle, hosted by the Duke, which started at seven thirty. Nora decided to grab some crisps and then get ready. Humphrey was due to pick her up at seven.

After eating some salt and vinegar flavoured crisps, Nora went up to her old bedroom. She was standing contemplating her costume when Heather arrived, tailed by their brother Milton.

"No chance we can come along?" Milton asked hopefully.

"I think all the tickets for the meal have been sold out but you can probably get tickets at the castle gates for the ball."

"Cool!" Milton grinned.

"You can go away while Heather helps me get into this thing." Nora told her brother.

"No problem." Milton shrugged and wandered off.

Heather closed the bedroom door.

"Do you think the Duke will ask you to dance?" She said as soon as the door was shut.

"Me? Unlikely."

"Likely." Heather corrected knowingly. "I bet he does. And then you'll leave at midnight and forget one of your shoes on the castle steps. And he will track you down to the bookshop, place it back on your foot and you'll live happily ever after."

"A Duke and a retail worker?" Nora scoffed.

"Bookshop manager." Heather corrected, unhooking the billowing renaissance dress. "Soon to be part *owner* with Cara. Two established antiquarian bookshops. Very tempting for a royal bibliophile."

"Georgina will never elope to the USA with Troy." Nora assured her sister.

"She talks about it a lot."

"I know." Nora chewed her bottom lip. "Well, if she does, then Cara and I have already discussed how we will go into business together and run both The Secondhand Bookworms. Georgina said she would sell it to us. I thought she might leave us in charge but she really does seem bent on selling it off and leaving the world of bookselling."

"Then it will be you in Castletown and Cara in Seatown." Heather said wistfully. "And you can go on calls together a couple of times a week."

"Hang on. You're forgetting about Humphrey." Nora then said as she shrugged out of her cardigan.

"Pfffft. You and Humphrey are more like best friends. With some kissing." Heather grinned.

Nora laughed, shaking her head.

"Have it all planned, do you?"

"Yep." Heather smiled. "Now let's get you ready for the Duke."

"For Humphrey." Nora corrected, smiling too.

"If you say so." Heather winked and unzipped Queen Elizabeth I.

Half an hour later, Nora was in the front room of the Jolly house, spinning slowly around in front of Wilbur, her elder brother, who had come round for dinner.

"Beautiful." He praised, fondly. "Are you going to behead some Catholics?"

"Queen Elizabeth I had Catholics *hanged, drawn and quartered.*" Nora corrected, stroking the stiff, lace ruff at her neck.

The front doorbell rang.

"I'll get it!" Heather called.

A moment later, the bloody vampire ghost of Sir Francis Walsingham was standing in the lounge. Humphrey wore an enormous white Elizabethan ruff, black doublet, hose, breeches and a heavy, velvet panelled black Elizabethan coat. He also had a fake but realistic beard and moustache, just like Sir Francis Walsingham's portrait. His eyes had been darkened with powder and his skin greyed and whitened like a ghost. He also had a pair of vampire fangs in.

"You both look awesome." Milton grinned, snapping photographs of Nora and Humphrey.

"Wow. I love the white face make-up." Humphrey told Nora.

"And the blood? I wasn't too sure about it." Nora asked, pointing to the sides of her mouth.

"You look like the gruesome vampire ghost of Queen Elizabeth I." Humphrey assured, smirking. "Let's go and hunt some Catholics."

"And suck their blood." Nora laughed, putting some vampire fangs in.

Humphrey did the same.

"Have a great time." Wilbur bade.

"Thanks." Nora took Humphrey's hand and they left the house to where a taxi was waiting outside.

"I did think about hiring us a horse drawn carriage, but it would take hours to get back to Castletown." Humphrey smiled, barring his fangs.

"This is fine." Nora laughed and they climbed in.

Nora leaned back, surrounded by so much fabric that she could hardly see Humphrey next to her. The taxi driver smirked at them in the mirror and then pulled away, setting off for Castletown and the Duke's Halloween Ball.

The Duke of Cole's castle was now closed from the end of October until the beginning of April. The ball was the last day that it would be open to the public. Since having the ruins of the ancient castle amalgamated into an impressive, grand, gothic New Castle almost two years ago, the new Duke had moved into his property and opened most of the house and grounds to visitors for half the year. He was renowned for his architectural skills and businesses, with vast estates throughout England and many wonderful and historic heirlooms.

The Duke's Halloween Ball was the first of its kind and had attracted plenty of dignitaries, including past mayors of Castletown, several royal relatives of the Duke, famous actors and actresses, wealthy residents from Castletown and surrounding towns as well as enthusiastic patrons of the castle.

The taxi dropped Nora and Humphrey at the castle gates where Georgina and Troy were waiting. Their costumes were brilliant. Troy made a very realistic Sweeny Todd and Georgina looked like a very scary Mrs Lovett, with a red striped dress and her apron covered in blood.

People in costume were visiting the Halloween Waxwork Museum by the gates, while others were entering the grounds, passing between the turreted walls and great sconces filled with real flames. The ticket collectors were dressed as ghostly noblemen. Nora, Humphrey, Georgina and Troy walked between the opened large iron gates and gave their tickets to one of the noble ghosts.

"Dinner in the Earl's Hall. This way please." He smiled and led the way to where a fleet of three wheeled haunted Tuk-Tuks were chauffeuring the guests up to the castle entrance. Nora stared in amazement. They were black and orange with cobwebs, bats and cats decorating them, the exteriors looped with battery-powered pumpkin lamps. They were being driven by skeleton drivers.

"Excellent." Humphrey grinned and took hold of Nora's hand, leading her to the first one.

They climbed aboard, Nora spread her billowing Elizabethan dress about her and the Tuk-Tuk set off along the winding path towards the Duke's castle. She leaned out of the doorway, watching the stunning grounds pass them by, gaze set upon the looming, many turreted castle ahead. She looked back, grinning to think of Sweeny Todd and Mrs Lovett following.

When the Tuk-Tuks reached the grand entrance, a skeleton footman offered Nora his hand. He helped her alight, she waited for Humphrey, Georgina and Troy to join her and they all climbed the magnificent stone staircase to enter the grand entrance hall.

Nora had already visited the castle twice, as a paying visitor to look around the areas opened to the public, and as a guest of the Duke's. The Duke had given Nora and Humphrey a private tour of his private library, so she had seen parts of the castle that only close friends of the Duke saw.

That evening, the castle seemed new and exciting, with stunning decorations, champagne fountains, brilliant lights and music floating down the many halls and corridors from the grand ballroom. The guests were directed towards the Earl's Hall, a grand, long room that had been restored by the Duke. When they entered through a high, oak doorway they were stunned at the magnificence of the enormous royal chamber.

An immense, long table ran the length of the hall, standing grandly in the centre and able to seat a hundred people. The walls were adorned with masterpiece paintings, there were choice antique heirlooms edging the walls beneath them with stunning heavy drapes either side of a long row of great, mullioned windows that overlooked part of the grounds and Castletown beneath. Nora hurried over to the window to seek out the areas where both The Secondhand Bookworm and her flat were located. She could just make them out.

A gong sounded and the many costumed guests were shown to their seats. Nora smiled to see Jeeves, the Duke of Cole's personal valet. He seemed to be searching for someone and when he saw her he headed over.

"Good evening Miss Jolly. Master Pickering." Jeeves bowed before Nora and Humphrey.

"Hello, Jeeves." Nora smiled.

Georgina and Troy watched with interest.

"You have been assigned specific seating this evening, Miss Jolly. Would both of you care to follow me?"

Nora and Humphrey looked at one another, grinned at Georgina and Troy and nodded, following Jeeves to seat closer to the head of the table. They were seated next to one another. Nora beside a dignitary in a soldier's uniform, Humphrey next to a famous actress dressed as Marie Antoinette. The actress admired Nora's costume and they chatted excitedly until it seemed all places were filled and the Duke of Cole was announced.

Nora peered eagerly over the head of the soldier and held her breath when she saw him. The Duke of Cole wore a magnificent medieval costume. He greeted people and he took his place at the head, smiling around the table. His gaze brushed with Nora's, held briefly in recognition, and then he cleared his throat.

"Good evening and welcome to my castle." The Duke smiled.

There was a round of applause and cameras flashed. Nora listened attentively as the Duke gave a welcoming speech, thanking everyone for supporting the charity of his choice which he revealed meant a lot to him personally. He had spent several years working with Aid to the Church in Need, especially assisting with Christians in Syria as well as spending 8 months in Iraq helping Christians returning to the Nineveh Plains. Nora gazed at the Duke with even deeper admiration as they sat down after his welcome and speech.

"Oh, and in case you were wondering," the Duke added, picking up his glass. "The costume I am wearing is of my ancestor, the Earl of Castletown, who was martyred for his Catholic Faith in Elizabethan England and whose shrine is housed in the Catholic Church in the town."

There were claps and comments of admiration before the dinner gong sounded, music began and the first course began to arrive.

"And such a handsome costume it is too." The actress leaned across Humphrey and said to Nora.

Nora glanced at her and nodded in agreement. They both smiled wistfully. Humphrey rolled his eyes.

Dinner in the Earl's Hall with the Duke of Cole was an event that would remain with Nora forever. As she made her way through five sumptuous courses, surrounded by the finest people in magnificent Halloween costumes, she would look occasionally at the Duke, handsome and sigh dreamily into her roast chicken, sherry trifle or goblet of wine. Sometimes she felt as though he was watching her, but whenever she looked down the table she saw him engaged in conversation with those closest to him or enjoying his meal.

Humphrey kept Nora's feet on the earth, entertaining her with impressions of a Vampiric Sir Francis Walsingham or chatting about family, work and other interests.

After dinner, everyone made their way through the fine halls and corridors to the enormous ballroom where guests who had not attended the dinner were already gathering. The ballroom was decorated with cobwebs, lanterns, lights and finery with a stage upon which sat an orchestra. A guest told the bookshop group that there were Glitter Angels hosting the event. Nora saw glitter angels with silver glittery skull faces, performing juggling or elegant dances about the room with cascades of glitter. Nora and Humphrey gathered with Georgina and Troy and dancing quickly began, peppered with speeches, announcements and special requests amidst glitter and music.

"Humphrey?!!!"

Nora almost choked on a canape as a petite blond witch stopped before them.

Humphrey slowly lowered his glass of wine.

"Jenny?!" He replied, agog.

"Yes! I can't believe it's you!" The pretty blond witch exclaimed and promptly threw her arms around him. "But I would recognise you anywhere. Even with that beard and moustache!"

Nora glanced at Georgina amused. Georgina was staring at Jenny.

"I can't believe it! Look at you. My goodness, you're so handsome." Jenny gushed, ignoring Nora who popped another canape into her mouth.

"And you. What are you doing here? I thought you were in Canada." Humphrey said, still staring at her agape.

"I returned last month."

"Did you marry?" Humphrey asked.

"No." Jenny smiled. "I still wasn't over a certain person."

They stared at one another meaningfully. Nora arched an eyebrow. As if finally remembering Nora, Humphrey glanced at her. Jenny had noticed Nora too and was giving her the evil eye.

"Oh. This is Nora. My…date." Humphrey said. "And you remember my sister? Georgina?"

"Georgina! Of course I do." Jenny said, playfully slapping Humphrey's arm.

He stood, grinning stupidly as Jenny and Georgina embraced.

Nora watched, moving back slightly as Humphrey, Jenny and Georgina began to reminisce. Georgina kept glancing at Nora, uncomfortably. Feeling completely forgotten and rather awkward, Nora edged politely away and watched them until she became aware of someone watching *her*.

Nora's gaze met with the Duke of Cole's. He was standing speaking with a group of people, his attention upon her. He seemed concerned. It seemed as though Humphrey had noticed the Duke's gaze and glanced at Nora sharply.

"We must catch up. Here's my mobile number." Jenny gushed.

She handed it to Humphrey who took it with a dashing smile, leaned in, kissed Jenny's cheek and muttered something to her. Nora felt her cheeks flame red.

Without even looking at Nora, Jenny headed off into the crowds. Humphrey moved back to Nora's side and took a sip of his wine, staring after Jenny. After a moment, Nora chuckled.

"Old girlfriend?" She teased.

"Yes." Humphrey replied.

Nora saw him staring at the Duke. She cleared her throat.

"Oh. Well you look very nice together. A lovely couple." She said lightly.

Humphrey looked at Nora with the perfect imitation of a vampire about to go for her throat.

"Like you and the Duke?" He asked flatly, barring his fangs, gulped down the rest of his wine and headed off into the crowd of people on the dance floor, leaving Nora staring after him, confused.

Georgina sidled up next to Nora.

"Jenny and Humphrey were engaged." She told Nora gently.

"Oh." Nora lost Humphrey's tall, Sir Francis Walsingham form as he disappeared behind a large man dressed as Frankenstein. "Why did they break up?"

"Jenny was offered a very good job in Canada. A year later she was getting married. Humphrey was very fond of her."

"I see." Nora said glumly.

"I'm telling you the truth so you can understand why Humphrey's acting like a typical man." Georgina sighed, shaking her head.

"Yes. I understand." Nora smiled. "I'm sure he's…"

Her words trailed off when she noticed Humphrey dancing with a petite, pretty blond witch. It felt as though a sudden stone had dropped into her stomach. Georgina noticed too and gasped.

"I'm surprised at him! The ass." She exclaimed.

"He's jealous of me and the Duke." Nora explained miserably.

"Pah! That's no excuse."

"I think I'll get some more wine." Nora decided and hurried away from the edge of the dance floor, stung by Humphrey's behaviour, but also feeling guilty. It wasn't a secret between them that she was fond of the Duke of Cole. But surely Humphrey wasn't taking that seriously. She turned and saw him still dancing with Jenny, pointedly ignoring Nora. Obviously he was taking it seriously. The jackass.

The sudden feeling of a hand on Nora's elbow made her jump.

Nora turned to see Jeeves standing politely next to her, holding a silver tray with a glass of white wine on it.

"Compliments of His Grace." Jeeves said.

"Oh." Nora stared at it. "Erm…th…thank you." She said and picked up the glass.

"And the napkin, Miss Jolly." Jeeves nodded.

Nora picked up the folded paper napkin that the glass had been standing on too as Jeeves gave her a pointed look, bowed and headed away.

She unfolded the napkin and her heart gave a small leap. Written in neat penmanship was a message. It read:

'Meet me in the library in five minutes. James.'

Nora took a large gulp of the wine, glanced over at the Duke who was seemingly oblivious as he spoke with a guest, and then considered Humphrey who was gliding around the dance floor with Jenny. Seeing Humphrey whisper something to Jenny, Nora immediately left the wine table, slipped out of the ballroom and found Jeeves waiting for her in the hall.

"This way, Miss Jolly." Jeeves said primly, although she noticed a slight smile curving his mouth.

"Thank you." Nora whispered.

Her heart was beating fast as she followed Jeeves through the hallways and corridors, up several flights of stairs, leaving the noise of the Halloween Ball far behind. She recognised the part of the castle that she had visited over the summer when given a tour of the Duke's private library by the Duke himself.

Jeeves led her to the door, opened it and gestured her inside.

The Duke's private library was magnificent. The Duke was a keen collector of subjects that interested him as well as a preserver of the many manuscripts and books he had inherited. He had special collections of mountain climbing and exploration books, cartography, classic and ancient history, antiquities and architecture. There were also rare letters, manuscripts and journals.

The books were housed in cases and most of the tomes were bound in leather, kept behind wooden and glass doors. Filigree woodworked arches with carved wooden pillars surrounded the centre of the room, supporting an upper gallery of books all around, even between the great arched, mullioned windows. In the centre of the private library, two enormous red velvet sofas faced one another with a walnut-wood coffee table in between. Six armchairs arranged with them faced a great stone inglenook fireplace that stood against the north wall. The carpets were rich, red striped with gold, and numerous lamps stood upon tables. The fire was alight.

"I shall bring a pot of coffee, Miss Jolly. His grace will join you shortly." Jeeves explained.

Nora looked at the valet, embarrassed.

"His Grace wishes to show you a new collection of books he has acquired. He tires quickly of guests and suspected you would like a little break from the Halloween festivities, too." Jeeves explained kindly.

Nora released a relieved breath.

"That is very considerate of his Grace. Thank you." Nora appreciated.

He bowed, smiled and left, leaving Nora alone in the library.

Nora gazed around, listening to the pleasant crackle of the fire. She glanced down at her magnificent Elizabethan dress, chuckled to herself and then heard the click of the door behind her as it closed. When she turned, His grace the Duke of Cole was staring at her.

After taking a small, quick breath, Nora's dropped her gaze.

"Good evening, Your Grace." Nora grinned, dipping into a small curtsey.

"Her majesty shouldn't curtsey to a mere Duke." The Duke smiled.

Nora chuckled.

"A wonderful Halloween party, Your Grace." Nora complimented.

He crossed the vast room, studying her thoughtfully. Nora noticed his gaze of concern.

"Thank you."

Nora understood from his expression that he had seen what had occurred between her and Humphrey. She felt her cheeks redden slightly.

"And thank you for joining me in the library." He stopped before her.

Nora looked up at his face.

"May I show you something?" He asked politely.

"Yes." Nora squeaked.

The Duke smiled, took hold of her hand and led her across the room to one of the ladders leading up to his gallery.

"Can you climb?"

"In this dress?"

"Yes."

Nora laughed.

"I shall try."

She hoisted up the fabric and began to climb the ladder, aware of the Duke ascending behind her.

"Oh. It's very high." Nora said, once they were at the top. She stood aside for him to step onto the wide, gallery floor and edged back as she stopped before her.

"You're very safe." The Duke assured her, pulling a small gate across the opening. "This way, please."

Nora walked with him, taking occasionally secret glances at his royal profile as he led her to a case.

"A new edition to my library." The Duke indicated.

Nora looked at the shelf.

"Your Grace! These are wonderful!" Nora exclaimed. "I did not know you were a lepidopterist."

The Duke grinned as Nora leaned closer and read a whole shelf of titles, books bound in leather, a serious and rare collection.

"Well, I find rare books with exquisite plates on butterflies of interest." He confessed.

"You mean, you don't go about the grounds with a butterfly net collecting specimens yourself?" Nora teased.

The Duke burst out laughing.

"Certainly not." He reached for a tome. "At least, not when anyone can see me."

Nora giggled, walking with the Duke as he took the book over to one of the small gallery tables. The book was called 'Butterflies collected in the Shire Valley, East Africa' and had been published in 1861. The plates were full colour, each page protected by tissue, exquisite condition and stunning. They bent over it for ages, discussing the production of such a book, before the Duke returned it to the shelf and gathered an armful of specific titles.

"We'll take them down. Jeeves has arrived with coffee. I'm not keeping you from the ball?" The Duke asked.

"No." Nora replied quickly.

The Duke gave a small smile.

"Nora. Do you mind if I ask you a question?"

They climbed down the ladder, Jeeves waiting at the bottom to ensure she didn't fall, and Nora took some of the books when she reached the bottom so the Duke could step down safely.

"No, of course not." Nora nodded. "Ask away."

"Thank you, Jeeves." The Duke said to his valet. Jeeves bowed and left.

They placed the Lepidoptera book on the coffee table. The Duke poured them both coffees, pondering Nora. She smiled at him.

"Thank you." She appreciated as he handed her a fine bone china cup and saucer, beautifully decorated. She took a sip. "Delicious. You wished to ask me a question, Your Grace?"

"James." He corrected.

Nora continued to sip her coffee, smiling.

"Yes." He nodded and sat down next to her.

Nora moved some of her dress fabric out of the way.

"Who was the little witch Humphrey was dancing with?" The Duke asked.

Nora almost choked on her coffee, hiding a laugh.

"Oh. You saw her?"

"You know I did." The Duke said softly.

Nora stared. She then cleared her throat.

"Her name is Jenny. She was Humphrey's serious love apparently."

"Are you not Humphrey's serious love?" The Duke asked.

Nora tried not to smile.

"Well. We have been dating for a while. There is a little affection between us. But nothing very serious."

She saw the Duke shuffle slightly.

"But," Nora continued thoughtfully, "I have to confess that I've always thought of Humphrey as a best friend."

The Duke smiled.

"Perhaps it would be fair to tell him that."

Nora examined her dress, intently.

"Yes. You're right. It would."

"So that, if someone else was interested in courting you, they would not think you were spoken for."

Nora felt her mouth go dry. She stared at the Duke, and then her lips twitched.

"Courting?" She asked, amused at his word choice.

He grinned.

"I am a *medieval* Duke." He reminded her, indicating his costume.

Nora laughed but she felt dazed.

"I visit the shrine of your ancestor each week." She then told him, deeming it wise to change the subject.

"At Mass?" He asked, interested.

"And sometimes I pop in during the week. The front pew on the right in the centre aisle is reserved for your family, Your Grace. I think it has been a tradition since your great, great, great uncle built the church."

"I had heard that." The Duke mused, sipping his coffee. "I attend Mass each week in London. Perhaps I should attend Mass in Castletown. Which Mass do you attend, Nora?"

Nora felt her cheeks reddening.

"Oh. The first Mass of the day."

The Duke took another sip of his coffee, smiling thoughtfully.

"You will be pleased to know," Nora then began, placing her cup and saucer carefully onto the coffee table and picking up a butterfly book, "that I came across a First Edition of the second Jeeves and Wooster book."

The Duke looked delighted.

"Really?"

Nora nodded.

"Carry on, Jeeves."

The Duke laughed.

"Is it in your shop?"

"Yes." Nora nodded.

"Then at a convenient time to you, may I purchase it?"

"Of course." Nora assured.

"Thank you." The Duke smiled, watching Nora pick up his 1908 copy of 'A history of British butterflies' by Rev Morris.

They perused the collection, discussing the plates and detailed information in the variety of tomes, reading sections aloud, admiring the covers and beautiful drawings and paintings. Nora particularly liked the

Duke's copy of 'Birds and Butterflies' by M G Musgrave.

The library door rapped politely.

"Your Grace. The glittery angel-women have informed me that they would like to do the confetti cannons and balloon drops, imminently, to conclude the Halloween Ball." Jeeves said.

The Duke checked his watch and looked surprised.

"How time flies." He said to Nora.

"When you're having fun." She concluded, standing up.

The Duke stood too.

"Thank you very much for showing me your new Lepidoptera book collection." She appreciated.

"You're very welcome." The Duke replied warmly.

Jeeves cleared his throat.

"May I walk you back?" He offered.

"Thank you." Nora nodded and they left the Duke's private library, tailed by Jeeves.

Nora slipped into the ball before the Duke, who waited a moment before making his way towards the stage. She spotted Humphrey, Georgina and Troy by the drinks table. Humphrey was nursing a glass of wine with a gloomy expression. He straightened up when he saw Nora approaching.

"Nora. Where have you been?" He asked, relieved.

"Looking at Lepidoptera." She replied with a friendly smile.

Humphrey looked blank. Georgina gave Nora a knowing smirk.

Before Humphrey could say anything else, people began to clap as the Duke of Cole mounted the stage, smiled at some glitter angels and took the microphone. Nora watched him as he announced the end of the ball, thanked everyone for coming, told them the final amount that had been raised for Aid to the Church in Need and then introduced the drumroll for the confetti canons and balloon drops.

Nora clapped loudly with everyone else as confetti and glitter descended around them from the high ceiling. People began to leave and the Duke made his way to the doors to shake everyone's hands, personally thank them and bid them a Happy Halloween.

"Did you have a nice evening?" Humphrey asked Nora miserably.

"I did." She said brightly.

He looked surprised.

"Did you?" She asked.

He shrugged, taking hold of Nora's hand.

Nora squeezed his fingers and nudged his arm with hers. He smiled guiltily so she shrugged as a way of telling him to forget about it.

"Sorry." He murmured in her ear as they neared the Duke.

The Duke saw them approaching and when they were in front of him he pondered Humphrey a moment before smiling.

"Humphrey."

"Your Grace." Humphrey nodded, bowing respectfully. "Happy Halloween."

The Duke took Nora's hand.

"Happy Halloween, Miss Nora Jolly." The Duke said formally.

Nora smiled.

"Good evening, Your Grace."

They moved along for Georgina and Troy to swoon over the Duke, before they walked with the crowd to the entrance doors and joined the fast-moving queue for the haunted Tuk-Tuks. Just before they climbed aboard, Jenny hailed 'goodbye', waving at Humphrey. Nora saw his face light up so she smiled thoughtfully to herself, gathered her Elizabethan dress, put in her vampire fangs and settled happily into the back of their Tuk-Tuk, her brain filled with glitter-angels, a five course meal, skeleton footmen and the Duke of Cole.

10 THE RAVENS AND THE TELL-TALE HEART

The following morning, Cara dropped Nora at the door of the flat on her way to the Seatown branch.

"Have a great day. Speak to you soon!" Cara called, honked the van horn and sped off, leaving Nora waving and unlocking her front door. Nora then gave a start as she faced the wall of boxes in her little hallway, piled up before her and containing fifty copies each of the six volumes of mystery detective novels by Father Enda Flood.

"I'd forgotten about you!" Nora said aloud, delighted, squeezed inside, closed the door behind her and picked up the top box.

It took Nora five minutes to carry all the boxes up her staircase and arrange them in her living room. She was sweating by the time she had finished so jumped into the shower, thinking over the Halloween Ball, the Duke of Cole and Humphrey. After a quick breakfast, Nora fed Beardie, stepped into her boots, ran down her stairs and was soon heading down the hill towards The Secondhand Bookworm.

It appeared that Hocus and Pocus were out and about early, doing their rounds drumming up business for their baby Halloween costumes. Halloween balloons and black spooky flags were appearing outside various shops. The street was more like 'Knockturn Alley' in the Harry Potter novels. Nora paused to look at the tall windows in the antique shops. Full skeletons were displayed in the bay window of one shop, with scary masks, animal skulls and shrunken heads in the other.

Stuffed owls in dioramas, cauldrons, carved pumpkins with horrible faces, huge jars filled with murky water and suspicious objects, different coloured jars and an assortment of spears filled the windows of other shops.

A woman who looked like the terrifying ghost from the movie 'The Ring' was standing outside the bank, handing out leaflets. She had lank, long black hair, brushed forward and a white, Victorian nightdress. As people passed by, she stuck an arm out and they warily took a leaflet. Nora stopped in front of her. She accepted a leaflet and read it aloud.

"The Castletown Halloween Monster Quest in Nineveh House. Ghoulish games, pumpkin carving, play a game of conkers or make a scary mask; hear a spine-chilling tale, create a dancing skeleton paper puppet and many more activities to make and take home. Saturday afternoon between two and five."

The woman looked up. She was Chinese so more like Sadako Yamamura from 'The Ring' *novels* than the actress from the 2002 movie. Nora blanched.

"Thank you. That sounds nice." Nora said, making to move away.

"Seven days!" A voice whispered in her ear.

Nora yelped loudly.

The Ring woman smirked, watching Nora turn to Harry who stood behind her, grinning.

"I couldn't resist." He confessed. "You should have seen your face. Great costume isn't it."

"Hmm." Nora agreed, grimly.

"Any new Beano or Dandy annuals? For my nephew?" He asked.

"No." Nora replied, spotting Betty heading down the hill.

"Call me if you get any? Neighbour."

"I will." Nora sighed, watching Harry head off to the delicatessen.

Since she had moved into her flat above the fudge shop in Castletown several months before, Harry had been delighted to be able to call Nora his neighbour. He lived in hope that she would call on him down Market Street to borrow a cup of sugar. They had first met when Harry had strolled into The Secondhand Bookworm dressed in black, with bulging muscles and black sunglasses and said 'I'll be back', thus earning him his nickname 'The Terminator'. Whenever Cara saw him in Seatown she skyped through to Nora: '*TERMINATOR ALERT!!*'

Sadly, now Nora only thought of him simply as Harry, although he often told her he would be back.

"Morning, Nora." Betty greeted, meeting Nora at the door of The Secondhand Bookworm.

"Morning, Betty." Nora grinned.

"I'm glad I'm not late. I thought I might be. Some old codger almost crashed into the back of me up the hill. I spotted a parking space and slowed down in good time but he must have been blind. Flippin' greyhead." Betty grumbled.

Nora unlocked the front door.

"Oh dear."

"There are still quite a few books to mark up, Nora." Betty said, regretfully.

Nora opened the door and flew across the room to turn off the alarm, grimacing at the two-toned door chime and glancing at the large pile of boxes of books to mark up by the window.

"Oh, that's okay." Nora said. "I can finish them off today."

"Cara said she left you all the Edgar Allen Poe books."

"Oh good. I like those." Nora admitted.

Betty quickly locked the door when a woman dressed as Charlie Chaplin tried to get in. She scowled when Betty pointed at the opening time, pointed to her pocket watch and decided to wait, twirling her cane.

"Ugh. These cobwebs are too realistic." Betty said, crossing the room.

"They are." Nora agreed, glancing in the direction of IT's house, which was still successfully sealed up, courtesy of Humphrey.

"I'll unlock the kitchen, pop the kettle on, priority, turn on the lights and check I didn't leave any hobos inside last night." Betty smiled.

Nora giggled.

"Okay. I'll fill up the till with the float and the open up for Ms Chaplin."

"Oh Nora. I do hope we aren't going to have a day of maddos." Betty lamented. "One man yesterday pinched my bottom."

"Really?! That's terrible."

"No. It was actually quite lovely." Betty winked, picked up the shop keys and set off to complete her chores.

Nora was smirking as she threw the money in the till, turned on the computer and decided to open up.

"Hello." She greeted the woman. "Charlotte Chaplin?"

The woman grinned.

"We're here for the costume parties tonight. You have a book in your window. A new copy of The Woman in Black? Can I take a look please? I'm going to see the play in Little Cove at The Jolly Theatre tomorrow."

"Are you? I'm going to see it tonight."

"Oh great!" Charlie Chaplin followed Nora inside.

"Yes. It's supposed to be terrifying." Nora said.

"Yes, I heard that. Awesome!"

Nora reached into the window display for one of the copies of the books and her hand froze. She had spotted a familiar couple crossing the road, eyes fixed on the bookshop. Her heart sank.

"It's good that you have new copies of the book." Charlie Chaplin was twittering.

"Hmm." Nora mumbled, handing it to her and peering through the window.

Mrs and Miss Raven were regulars to The Secondhand Bookworm. Mother and daughter, they collected children's books, conversed in whispers, paid in small change, carried mountains of carrier bags and demanded a ten percent discount and lots of bookworm bags even for single Ladybird Book purchase.

Nora returned to behind the desk as Betty emerged through the walkway that led into the stairwell and back room.

"Kettle's on." She said, brightly.

"Bad news." Nora mumbled, nodding to the door as Miss Raven loomed up to it, stood on the threshold and stared into the room.

"Oh great." Betty muttered sarcastically. She then smiled glamorously as Charlie Chaplin handed her the copy of The Woman in Black.

"This please." Charlie Chaplin said.

"Oh, how wonderful! Such an excellent book. Have you read it?" Betty asked.

"No. I'm going to see the play tomorrow."

"Oh how exciting for you. We are going tonight as a bookshop trip."

Nora watched Miss Raven enter the shop followed by her plump mother and accompanied by a retinue of rustling plastic bags. They headed for the window, whispering loudly. Once Charlie Chaplin had left, Miss Raven turned to Nora and Betty.

"Hello." She said, smiling widely.

"Hello, Miss Raven." Nora smiled back.

"Ah, you have a couple of books in your window. May we have a look?"

"Of course. Which ones are they?"

Nora moved around the counter and stopped by the window. Mrs Raven stared at her.

"Are they all priced?" Mrs Raven asked in a loud whisper.

"Yes, all the books are priced." Nora nodded.

"May...we...have...a...look?" Mrs Raven then asked breathlessly.

She was wheezing and puffing, as if she had asthma or allergies.

"I just asked the young lady, poppet!" Miss Raven said shrilly.

Nora cleared her throat.

"Which books are you interested in?"

"'The Face in the Frost', 'The Mummy, the Will and The Crypt', 'The Bell, the Book and the Spellbinder' and 'The Vengeance of the Witch-Finder'. Four John Bellairs children's books." Miss Raven said sweetly.

Nora hid a scowl as she began to move books aside to reach for them. She had been pleased with her John Bellairs display and always felt annoyed when the Ravens came in and swiped the children's books from the window display. Once she had reached them, Nora passed each book to Miss Raven. She then left the Ravens bent over the books, whispering.

On her way back to the counter, Nora picked up a box of Edgar Allen Poe books to price up. She pulled a face at Betty who rolled her eyes at the Ravens.

"I'll make us some tea, Nora." Betty said and headed back to the kitchen.

While the Ravens huddled over the books, another customer arrived. He was big and beefy and wore a grey t-shirt with a picture of a grinning pumpkin on the front with the words 'Let's get smashed!' He was followed by Crossword Lady who was smiling mildly and clutching her morning paper.

"Have you got any tissues?" The man asked.

"Erm…not for sale." Nora replied.

"One of your own then?" He asked hopefully. "My nose is running."

Nora hid her grimace as she dove under the counter to search for the staff box of tissues. She found it and offered it to him as Crossword Lady stopped at the counter.

"Thanks." Beefy-Man appreciated.

He swiped one and left, blowing his nose like a clown's horn.

"Hello, Gina." Crossword Lady greeted.

"Hello." Nora replied politely.

"Another literary clue. Can you help me?" She asked, unfolding her paper.

Miss and Mrs Raven where arguing now in whispers. Miss Raven threw one of the books on the floor in a temper.

"I'm…just…saying…you…can…have…three." Mrs Raven whispered breathlessly.

"I want them all, Poppet!" Miss Raven hissed back.

Nora ignored them.

"Now. The Halloween literary question." Crossword Lady continued.

Another man arrived. He wore a gruesome green Halloween sweater with the words: I don't do costumes. Now step aside, you're treading on my invisible dog.'

Nora snorted on a laugh.

"The question. 'House of (blank), debut novel by Mark Z. Danielewski?" Crossword Lady asked.

Nora paled.

"House of Leaves." She said and shuddered. "Oh, that is a terrifying book. It's ergodic literature, filled with notes, pictures, drawings, scribbles and some pages only contain a few lines of text. The story is quite unnerving. It's in first person narrative and is about doors appearing in a house which contain massive Cathedral-like spaces that then go on forever. I'm telling you this because I read it and wish I never had!"

"Leaves. Yes, that fits perfectly. Thank you, once again. What a great find you are." Crossword Lady said, filling in her crossword. "I hope to see you at the Critters Stall tomorrow."

"I'll try." Nora said politely.

"Goodbye, Gina. I must say, you are doing a long stint of research for your next movie role. I look forward to seeing the film. I assume it's set in a bookshop?"

Nora stared at her blankly.

Finally she said 'yes', so Crossword Lady smiled happily and left.

The man with his invisible dog stopped before Nora.

"Gina. Have you got a café here, like in Waterstones in Piertown?" He asked.

"Oh, my name isn't Gina, it's Nora. That lady thinks I am an actress and won't believe me when I tell her I'm not." Nora explained.

The man laughed.

"How funny."

"In answer to your question. We don't have a café."

"But those are cups of tea." He said, pointing to Betty who arrived carrying their refreshments. Betty stared.

"Yes. But they're from our pokey little staff kitchen." Nora replied.

"Huh. Any other bookshops in town where I can sit and browse while drinking a cappuccino?"

"I'm afraid not." Nora assured.

The man sighed.

"Okay. I don't suppose I can bring a take-away tea inside and squat somewhere to read?" He asked.

"No." Nora assured.

"Thanks." He said glumly, turned and left.

Nora and Betty looked at one another. Betty was about to make a sarcastic comment when Mrs and Miss Raven walked up to the counter.

"Yes. I would like to purchase these three books. Can you keep this one by for me please?" Miss Raven asked, angrily.

"Oh. Erm…yes of course." Nora nodded.

"Ask her if...ask her if…" Mrs Raven was whispering.

Miss Raven ignored her.

"We would like to have a look upstairs. May we leave our bags?" She asked, threateningly.

"Erm…"

"It would really help us!" Miss Raven hissed, blue eyes flashing.

"Er…okay."

Betty almost ran for cover as Mrs and Miss Raven sped around the counter to deposit their mounds of bags. Nora glared. They then shuffled off, creaking up the first flight of stairs while arguing spitefully in whispers.

"Horrid bags." Betty said, not referring to the ones they had deposited.

"I know. They've messed up my window display. Guess I'll just have to price up these Edgar Allen Poe books and put them in the window. Oh, there are some lovely editions here. This one is illustrated by Arthur Rackham." Nora said, picking a book from the box.

"Oh, that is lovely, Nora. And you will make a wonderful window display." Betty said. She was touching her stomach tentatively and Nora noticed.

"Are you feeling alright, Betty?"

"Oh, my stomach is still a little sensitive. I had an awful night, Nora. I went on a date with Emmett, you know, the one my daughter set me up with, the ancient old greyhead who looks like a turtle. And after dinner he asked me to sleep over. At first I thought he wanted to seduce me, he's so OLD Nora that the thought didn't excite me, but I agreed anyway and he drove me back to his large house. It was so cold, Nora, and the selfish old miser refused to turn on any heating. We sat in his lounge drinking hot milk and twice he fell asleep on me, with his head lolling back and his mouth wide open, snoring like a pig."

Nora choked with laughter on her tea.

"In the end I told him I wanted to go to bed. I thought he might get some funny ideas and molest me but I wasn't that lucky." Betty continued, her eyes twinkling. "He put me up in a smelly old guest bedroom and it was like sleeping in a freezer. I thought he wanted me to experience what it'll be like in a morgue. Then obviously what we had eaten for dinner didn't agree with me because I started to get such wind. I had such pains in my stomach Nora, and I had to let rip. And it was so loud, for a good few hours. I thought Emmett must have heard me. I sounded like a brass band. But in the morning he didn't say anything, he *is* quite deaf. I came straight to work and have decided to dump him."

Nora's eyes were wet with laughter tears.

"Oh dear. Oh dear." Nora said, bent over laughing.

"Thanks for listening." Betty appreciated, smirking.

It took Nora about five minutes to stop giggling and by that time the Ravens had returned.

Miss Raven was carrying two Ladybird books with both hands. Mrs Raven was following with a little plastic bank bag full of coins in her cupped hands. Nora quickly picked a book from her Edgar Allen Poe box and jumped when she saw that it was a copy of 'The Raven'. She quickly hid it.

"Those ones for you?" Betty asked politely, reaching for the books.

"This one is priced a little too high." Miss Raven said, gripping tight.

"Oh dear." Betty replied, flatly.

"I wonder if you could take a little off. There is a squashed daddy-longlegs in the back."

"Squashed spiders are extra." Betty laughed.

Miss Raven kept a straight face.

"May I take a look?" Nora asked.

Reluctantly, Miss Raven passed it to her.

Nora opened the book nervously. There was indeed the body of a squished spider, but it was only a baby one. She checked the price and repressed a sigh. It had only been marked at a pound.

"I can do it for ninety pence." Nora said.

Miss Raven's smile faltered.

"Not less? It is after all, a corpse."

"There'll be another corpse in here in a minute." Betty muttered into her tea.

Nora tried not to laugh.

"I can knock ten pence off. And with your ten percent discount I believe it will be a fair price."

"Fine!" Miss Raven smiled with gritted teeth.

"Ask her if...ask her if...." Mrs Raven whispered.

"I KNOW!" Miss Raven whispered back, glaring at her mother. She turned back to Nora and smiled. "I wonder, may we have these books in a separate bag to the John Bellairs books we wish to buy?"

"No problem." Nora said, not even bothering to argue.

"Thank you so much. It helps us so much." Miss Raven said, pleased and looked at her mother.

As if on cue, Mrs Raven emptied her entire bag of coins on the cash book. Two pence pieces and tiny five pence pieces rolled in all directions. Nora and Betty helped collect them all and then the Ravens counted the money out in whispers while Nora rang the prices through the till and Betty unhooked two bright blue plastic bags while swearing under her breath.

A man stepped into the shop smiling. He had a trimmed ginger beard and wore a t-shirt that read: 'This is the best costume. Believe me it's tremendous. If you say it's just a t-shirt you're fake news'. Nora recognised him as one of the actors from Seymour's theatre. His name was Alex.

Alex gave Nora joyful wave and headed into the back. She heard him creaking up the stairs and walking into the front room so she assumed he was looking at the plays section.

"Thank you." Miss Raven said when Nora passed the two, almost empty, large carrier bags to her.

The Ravens then gathered their mountain of other bags from behind the counter, whispering and elbowing each other. Betty was almost pushed into the computer. Finally they left, leaving Nora and Betty shaking their heads in disgust.

A blood-curdling scream then sounded, announcing a text message had arrived on Nora's phone.

"Oh Nora. What was that?" Betty asked, worried.

Nora held up her iPhone.

"Sorry. That was me."

"Oh that's alright. I thought it might be the ghost of the boy down the well."

Nora's smile faded.

While Betty dealt with a group of old ladies wishing to purchase postcards (the spinners were still inside), Nora saw with a flutter of her heart that the message was from the Duke of Cole. She opened it breathlessly.

'Morning, Nora. I wonder, would you care to have lunch with me this afternoon? I can bring a tray down to your garden and I could also purchase 'Carry on, Jeeves'? Yours, James.'

Nora swallowed hard. She then began to type.

'Hello, Your Grace. I would very much like that. I can meet you in my garden and bring with me the copy of 'Carry on, Jeeves'. It is priced at sixty five pounds. – Nora'

She pressed send and waited.

A moment later:

'Wonderful. Is one o'clock a good time for you?'

'Perfect.'

'I look forward to seeing you then, Nora.'

'See you later, Your Grace.'

'James.'

Nora smiled, paused and then wrote his name. She stared at it for a long time and then pressed send before she could change her mind. Smiling to herself, Nora waited until Betty had finished moaning about how ugly and rude one of the ladies buying postcards was before asking:

"Can I go for lunch at one o'clock? I'm meeting someone."

"Of course, Nora. Oh, how lovely for you." Betty said happily. "Is it Humphrey?"

"No." Nora shook her head.

She then picked up the copy of 'The Raven' and began to price up the book quickly.

Betty was watching Nora thoughtfully, and then smiled, picking up a book to price too.

"These books are lovely." Nora said, examining a copy of 'The Tell-Tale Heart'.

"Oh they are, Nora." Betty agreed.

"I like these illustrations by Harry Clarke on Edgar Allen Poe's 'Tales of Mystery and Imagination'." She said.

"Oh they are wonderful." Betty nodded.

"I think I'll put this one in the window display." Nora decided, standing up.

She walked over to the window and then jumped. Sadako Yamamura from 'The Ring' was staring demonically into the shop through the front side window. She then smiled, waved and headed off. Nora shook her head.

Alex returned with a pile of plays.

"Morning, Nora!" He greeted cheerfully.

"I like your t-shirt." Nora grinned.

Alex chuckled, passing the books to Betty who gave him a look and winked at Nora.

"Seymour is having us all practice the plays lined up for November." Alex explained, referring to Seymour's troupe. "I thought I'd get a head start and rehearse some. You had them upstairs."

"That's a good idea." Nora smiled. "Have you seen The Woman in Black yet?"

"Yes. I was able to be an understudy for the main character."

"Wow. What's he like in real life?"

"Down to earth. Really nice. They are both exceptional actors, which is why they've been so successful in stage and screen. Seymour's had his troupe watching them rehearse and then be present at several of the performances. We've learned a lot."

"What play has Seymour chosen for Christmas this year?" Nora asked.

"Magic by G K Chesterton." Alex replied.

Nora chuckled.

"Seymour loves his Chesterton." She grinned.

Alex paid, chatted for a bit and then headed off, leaving Nora and Betty continuing to price books while serving lots of Shriek-Week customers.

At five to one, Nora left Betty displaying the last of the Edgar Allen Poe books and set off up the hill to her flat. In the summer Nora had discovered a locked door in the wall backing onto the Duke's estate. The Duke was her landlord and he had shortly after revealed to her that he had the key. It opened from the outside in. Nora had many dreams and fantasies about meeting the Duke in her garden. Now they were coming true!

Access to her garden on her side was through a small corridor between Nora's staircase and the Fudge Pantry. The corridor turned left under her staircase and then was a narrow run down to a heavy, windowless door. When she had first moved in she had had to get Humphrey to clear away real cobwebs as well as about one hundred resident spiders. She had then swept it, painted the walls, replaced the single, dirty lightbulb with a lovely new bright one, put down some rugs and hung up some pictures. It was now a pleasant walk to the garden.

Once she was inside, Nora cleared some leaves from her little iron table, placed the wrapped First Edition 'Carry on, Jeeves' on top, topped up the bird feeder, positioned her pumpkin she had bought at The Pumpkin Shop with Georgina and placed on the floor onto a small box ready for carving on Saturday night and then heard a knocking on the outer door.

The passionflower vine that concealed the door was thick and heavy, devoid now of flowers and fruit. Since it was on the north facing wall, it was able to catch strong sunlight over the summer that peeped over the top of the building from the south. Nora went over, knocked back and then heaved the vine aside as the door unlocked and opened. The Duke of Cole stepped in, helping her move the vine away with a grin.

"Good afternoon, Nora." He greeted.

"Your Grace." Nora curtseyed, grinning back.

"James." He corrected in a murmur, standing aside to allow Jeeves to enter behind him.

Jeeves was carrying a large silver tray. On it rested a teapot, sugar bowl, jug of cream, small silver tier of crust-less sandwiches, stack of small ceramic plates and two covered dishes of cake. Nora stared, amazed.

"Good afternoon, Miss Jolly." Jeeves nodded.

"Hello, Jeeves." Nora smiled, indicating towards the table.

The Duke peered around, admiring the garden.

"Thank you." Nora appreciated, helping Jeeves put down the tray.

"What time do you go back to the bookshop, Nora?" The Duke asked.

"I have half an hour for lunch." Nora replied.

Jeeves nodded, bowed, smiled at the Duke and set off out of the garden, closing the door behind him. The Duke turned to Nora. He held up the key. Nora reached out and took it.

"Wow. Is it gold?"

"Highly polished iron." The Duke smiled.

"What are these decorations? Oh! They're passionflowers." Nora realised, examining the intricate metalwork. "Hmm. I think this garden has a history."

"Apparently it does. I discovered a journal in my library in my home in Norfolk. A great, great, great aunt of mine would stay with the last Duke who lived here in Castletown, before the fire that burned down the former castle, over one hundred and eighty years ago. She tells of a romance the Duke had with a young lady who was a tenant of this very property."

Nora bit back a smile.

"Is that true?"

"On my honour." The Duke assured, eyes twinkling.

Nora arched an eyebrow.

"Did they plant the passionflower vine?"

"There is mention of it in the journal." The Duke said, watching Nora thoughtfully.

"What a lovely story." She smiled, handing him back his key.

"And ironic." The Duke said.

Nora bit back a smile.

"Are we having a romance then, Your Grace?" She dared to tease.

He looked at her intensely, but gave a rueful smile.

"How is Humphrey?" He asked, gesturing to the table.

They walked over and sat down. The Duke began to arrange the teacups. Nora poured a dash of milk into one, and, at a nod from the Duke, poured a splash of milk into his. He then poured a stream of hot, golden tea into each.

"I expect he is well." Nora finally replied.

Before the Duke could question her further, she held up the book.

"Carry on, Jeeves." She said.

The Duke grinned and took it eagerly.

"Thank you. I did enjoy the first one. I shall start this tonight."

Nora watched him take the book out of the plastic wrapping, open it and flick through the pages with a smile. She realised her heart was pounding so hard that she wondered if the Duke could hear it, like the narrator in Edgar Allen Poe's 'The Tell-Tale Heart'.

"Have you read this?" The Duke asked her, placing it down beside the lunch tray.

Nora nodded.

"Then may we discuss the first one?"

"Like in a book club?" Nora asked, thoughtfully.

The Duke smiled.

"Absolutely." He nodded, meeting her eyes, warmly.

Nora's heart began to pound again, as violently as the murdered old man in 'The Tell-Tale Heart. She cleared her throat, looking for any sign that the Duke could hear it. Then, with a smile she picked up her tea and took a sip, deciding that he would understand, after all, it wasn't every day that a bookshop girl got to sit down and have lunch with a Duke!

11 THE WOMEN IN BLACK

When Nora returned to The Secondhand Bookworm, Betty had been run off her feet. She showed Nora the cash book, complaining about one man who looked like he was constipated and another who smelt of beetroot.

"Did you have a nice lunch, Nora?" Betty asked, shrugging into her puffy coat.

"Lovely." Nora sighed wistfully. She then cleared her throat and turned to a customer who entered the shop.

The man wore a t-shirt that had a cartoon of two bees with ghost sheets over their heads and speech bubbles with them saying 'boo!' Underneath them in large letters it said: 'Show me your boo-bees'. Nora's eyebrows shot up. Betty nudged Nora and pointed to herself questioningly. Nora smothered a laugh.

"I'll just pop to the delicatessen for some bread. It might settle my stomach." Betty said and headed off.

"Love the decorations." Bee-man said.

"Thanks." Nora smiled, trying not to look embarrassed by his t-shirt.

"Hocus Pocus, I need coffee to focus." He then said. Nora smiled.

"Do you have any Mark Twain novels?" He then asked.

"If we did they would be in the attic room."

"Oh. You have an attic?"

"Yes. Through there and up the stairs."

"Thanks." The man smiled and headed off.

"Heeeellooooo, Nora." A familiar voice then said.

Nora turned back to the doorway to see White-Lightning Joe. He was on the step, looking hopeful.

"Hello." Nora replied.

"Guess I'm still banned." He pouted.

"Sorry, but yes."

He followed the curve of his downturned mouth with both index fingers of his hands.

"I've stopped stealing books." He assured her.

"It's not my shop. Georgina's in charge." Nora said.

"Did you speak to Seymour?" He asked.

Nora nodded.

"Pop to the Jolly Theatre one morning at ten o'clock and he'll interview you." She relayed.

White-Lightning Joe gasped.

"Really Nora? Thanks! I will. Do you want to get a drink?"

Nora glowered.

"No."

"Oh. Eeeeeep. Sorry, misread the signs. Okay. Well, I'd better go before Georgina catches me. Bye, Nora. Bye. Eeeeeeek."

He almost fell in the shop as a large man tried to pass by him. Nora wanted to laugh at the look of horror on White-Lightning Joe's face as his arms flayed about like a windmill. He steadied himself, turned and ran off. The large man stomped inside, scattering leaves and rubbish that had dropped onto the mat.

"Where's this well then?" He demanded.

"What?" Nora asked.

"The Red Plaque says you have the ghost of a boy down a well in here. *Well*. Where is it?"

Nora grimaced.

"Under the flagstones." She pointed.

The man looked. He then walked over, got down onto his hands and knees and stuck his ear to the floor. Nora stood up to stare at him.

"Well, well, well. I hear him. I swear I hear him." He nodded.

When he stood up he had bits of floor fluff and a leaf in his hair. Nora didn't mention it.

"Thanks." He said, turned around and left.

The sound of a fanfare announced the arrival of a Skype chat message on the computer. Nora turned and saw that it was from Roger.

'Customer request. 'The Cuckoo's Calling: Cormoran Strike Book One' by Robert Galbraith, aka J K Rowling – waiting – Roger'

'Can't look at the moment as Betty is on lunch.'

'Boo and hiss to you!'

Nora made a note to look when Betty was back and watched the haunted Tuk-Tuk head up the hill. A moment later a man in a pinstriped suit with curly blond hair biked up to the door. He got off his bike, folded it up and brought it into the shop, smiling.

"Hello." He greeted.

"Hello, Charles." Nora smiled.

Charles was a regular who collected old books, especially early editions of classic novels. He worked in the town and popped in occasionally to see what new arrivals there were.

"Oh. Very Halloween-themed." He said, looking at the decorations.

"Yes. Thought we'd get into the spirit of things."

"Well, you certainly have." He said. "Mind if I have a browse?"

"Go ahead." Nora smiled and watched Charles lean his bike by the door and then join her behind the counter where he spent ages examining all the antiquarian and rare book shelves.

"Oh. A 1909 edition of The Fairy Tales of the Brothers Grimm, illustrated by Arthur Rackham." He said, picking up a large, thick hardback book.

"The plates in that are beautiful." Nora nodded.

Charles whistled.

"Three hundred and fifty pounds." He read.

"Are you tempted?"

"Not if I wish to remain married to my wife." Charles grinned. "Ah, this one is published by Constable and Company Ltd. It was originally published by Freemantle in 1900 but Constable purchased the copyright and reissued this sumptuous version with the illustrations redrawn, revised and recoloured. Jacob and Wilhelm Grimm wrote twisted tales of cannibalism, mutilation, infanticide and sorcery. Imagine having these read to you every night as a child. Your blood would have run cold."

"Aesop's Fables are bad enough." Nora agreed. "Oh, have you read Hillaire Belloc's Cautionary Tales for Children?"

"Jim: Who ran away from his nurse, and was eaten by a lion." Charles quoted with a smirk.

"Henry King: Who chewed bits of string, and was early cut off in dreadful agonies." Nora recalled.

"Godolphin Horne: Who was cursed with the sin of pride, and, became a boot-black." Charles remembered.

Nora giggled.

"Lord Lundy: Who was too freely moved to tears, and thereby ruined his political career." Charles added.

"Rebecca: who slammed doors for fun and perished miserably." Nora said.

Charles laughed, shaking his head.

"Oh dear. The things we tell our children." He mused.

"I shall be reading 'The Gashlycrumb Tinnies' to some children tomorrow." Nora revealed.

Charles found that very amusing.

The arrival of the window cleaner distracted them both for a moment. He was noisy and clattered about with his ladder before washing all the windows and the new door window. The Castletown window cleaner was deaf, so when he had finished he came in to collect his payment and stuck his thumbs up at Nora cheerfully. She stuck her thumbs up as a thank you and he grinned, heading off.

After Charles had left, having resisted buying anything, Betty returned. Nora ran up to look for the Robert Galbraith book for Roger but had no luck. The shop was a bit of a tip, with leaves and fluff on all the floors and books thrown in corners. She went back up with the broom and dustpan and brush and swept out the entire shop and stairs. Then she replied to Roger that she couldn't find his book request.

The Cat-Man popped in. He had orange hair and collected books about cats, mainly any Louis Wain. He had a browse, said he was off to the pub for a tipple and left. After the Gorey-ent Express had made its appearance in the square, deposited a group of witches and several zombies and left a trail of puffy green smoke that entered the door and filled up the whole room, Nora and Betty spent the rest of the afternoon serving customers and making rude comments about them.

"Where are your free maps of Castletown?" A man with a Scream mask on asked.

"You have to open the map out and it's in the inside." Nora explained for the millionth time.

He unfolded the free map noisily and shook his head. "It's tiny!"

"The town is pretty much tiny." Nora defended.

"Pffft." The man said and left.

A man with a t-shirt that had a picture of a ghost on it with the phrase 'Let's get sheet-faced' bought two bags of Folio Society books. Nora rearranged the shelves and asked Seatown via Skype if they had any decent Folio Society books to send over.

'Get your own!' Roger replied rudely.

'We could do with about ten. NICE ones.' Nora insisted.

'I suppose I could sort some out for you.'

'Thanks!'

Betty gave Nora a look.

A blood-curdling scream informed Nora that a text message had arrived. Betty went to fetch Henry the hoover from the kitchen to clean the front of the shop, so Nora sat and opened the message. It was from Humphrey.

'Still on for me to pick you up tonight at seven? Xxx'

Nora thought about that.

'Sure. Georgina wants us women to wear black! x'

She sent back.

'I hope she doesn't expect me to wear a dress!' Humphrey replied.

Nora laughed.

The last customer of the day was a regular customer called Eugene. He was a local author whose books about sites where interesting buildings once stood often amused Nora. They were full of photographs of empty fields and waffling information. He had a beanie hat squashed on his head and many warts on his face.

Nora knew him outside The Secondhand Bookworm from her astronomy club.

"Hello, Nora." He said formally.

"Hello, Eugene." She replied.

"Mars is in perfect visibility this weekend." Eugene told her. "Are you going down to Little Cove beach on Sunday night?"

"Yes." Nora smiled. "The Orionids peak this week too."

"Twenty meteors are visible every hour." Eugene nodded.

"Did you see the Draconids?" Nora asked.

"Yes. The new moon allowed us to see the meteorites very clearly. Would you like me to autograph this book for you?"

"Oh." Nora stared at one of Eugene's local history books. "Have you not signed it already?"

"No." He said, walking over to the counter. "I see David Bone has pride of place."

Nora grimaced. All local authors complained about Georgina's support of Dave Bone's new local history guides.

"Well, if you sign your book I'll put it on top of David Bone's." Nora said.

Eugene smiled, signed it and went back to browse the Cole section.

Nora quickly covered up David Bone's books.

Hugh the street sweeper stopped outside the shop and peered in through the doorway.

"Not many customers then?" He pointed out.

"We've been busy today." Nora said, irritably.

"Sure you have." Hugh smirked rudely. "Was it you that left the dog's mess up the hill?"

Nora stared.

"What?"

"Near your flat. A big dollop of dog's mess. Took me ten minutes to clear it."

"No! I don't even have a dog."

"Hope it wasn't human then." He shrugged, gave her an accusing look and left.

Nora shook her head, amazed at his insolence.

"Insolent." She muttered.

Betty wheeled Henry noisily into the front room.

"I've soaped the kitchen so it's not a pigsty out there anymore." She said.

"Oh well done." Nora smiled.

She was googling the name 'Bellerophon Books' again, something she did regularly in a quest to discover a mysterious bookshop supposedly located in Castletown. People often asked if The Secondhand Bookworm was Bellerophon Books. So far, Nora hadn't discovered anything. She thought about hiring a P.I.

"Would you like me to hoover?" Nora offered.

"Oh thank you Nora, but no, don't worry, I'm not too ancient to whiz this sexy red Henry around the shop." Betty assured.

Nora giggled.

"Oh. A message from Seatown from Cara. Sage software lessons with Devon the accountant will start in November." She then read.

"Oh honestly, Nora. Does Georgina really think I'll be able to understand accounting software when I have trouble enough checking the emails?" Betty grumbled and plugged in the hoover.

"It's a six week course." Nora added.

"Bah!" Betty moaned, switched on Henry and began to hoover up giant leaves, which clogged the pipe for a full eight minutes.

Georgina had organised the lessons with Devon in the hope that her full-time and part-time members of staff would be able to fill in the spreadsheets over the year to save Cara lots of work preparing the accounts. Nobody was happy about it.

Nora and Betty finally locked up at five o'clock. It appeared that the pumpkin candles in the window had run out, so while Betty cashed up, Nora replaced the batteries and rearranged them under the watchful eye of a zombie who was peering in through the window.

"I'm so looking forward to this play." Betty said as they locked the door.

Nora had left the free map box out under the blind in front of the bay window, in the hope that visiting zombies would clear them out of the pesky things.

"I'm not." Nora admitted. "Seymour has billed it as the most terrifying play in the world."

"Well, it is supposed to be." Betty nodded.

"Are you dressing in black?"

Betty pulled a face.

"I'll look like a hideous old witch, Nora. But I suppose I shall." She glowered.

"The men are wearing black suits." Nora added.

"Oh but they'll all look handsome." Betty sighed.

They started up the street together, passing a knot of people on a Haunted Castletown Walking Tour, examining the Halloween window displays and finally parting at Nora's flat.

Nora dressed in an ankle-length black skirt and a Steampunk black blouse, with frills and flowing cuffs. It was open at the throat, with a black choker trimmed with lace and an elegant drop of brass cogs and wheels. She pulled her hair up into a bun and added a brass dragon brooch to her blouse. She then stepped into some black boots and shrugged into a short black ladies tailcoat with lovely brass buttons.

Cara was a serious Steampunk fan and favoured corsets. They had both dressed up for several Steampunk parties, so Nora thought her outfit was near enough Victorian and suitable for the Woman in Black. To finish off her get-up she popped a ladies black top hat with a lace veil and pheasant feather in the band on her head.

She then spent twenty whole minutes admiring herself until Humphrey arrived.

"You look amazing!" Humphrey gawped, stepping aside for Nora to exit her flat.

"Thanks." Nora chuckled, locking her door. "I love the suit."

"It's boring compared to your outfit."

"Swapsies?" Nora asked.

Humphrey laughed.

"Listen," he linked his arm with hers, walking her to his car, "it's not still weird between us is it? After my idiotic behaviour with Jenny at the ball last night."

"No." Nora shrugged, not meeting his eyes.

"Good. Because I was just jealous about you and the Duke of Cole." Humphrey assured.

"Don't be daft." Nora said and climbed into his van quickly.

Humphrey closed the door, looking at Nora through his windshield as he walked around the front of the van to the driver's seat. Nora hid behind a face compact and did her make-up.

The drive to Little Cove only took ten minutes. Humphrey found a good parking spot close to the theatre and they walked down the street to the Art Deco theatre which was teeming with people and buzzing with conversation.

Seymour had had the theatre decorated for Halloween. It was gothic and very atmospheric, with black chandeliers, flickering wall sconces, tattered drapes, cobwebs and a flow of dry ice making the floor seem like a graveyard at night. He had had the walls hung with Halloween tapestries that made the large entrance hall look like a magnificent haunted house.

"Nora. Humphrey!" Cara called.

The Secondhand Bookworm party had gathered by the main staircase and were all hailing them.

"Hello!" Nora greeted, hugging Cara, Georgina and then her sister Heather, who all looked amazing in Steampunk dresses with black veils. Betty was already there and wore a black skirt, black blouse and a hat with a veil. She was glowering.

"We're spread between two boxes." Georgina explained. "Next to each other and opposite the royal box."

"Great." Nora nodded, gazing around at the crowd.

An announcement was made and Seymour arrived, grinning.

"I can't wait to hear you all scream." He said.

"Torturer." Heather grinned, prodding him in the back as he led the way to the boxes.

"Here. Programmes to share out." Seymour said as Alex arrived holding a stack.

"Hello, everyone." Alex greeted cheerfully. "Jacob and Danny will be taking drink orders. There's a new upper level bar now so we can serve the guests better on the upper levels."

"That sounds great!" Cara grinned.

Danny, a theatre usher, knew the Jolly siblings well. Nora sidled up to Seymour.

"Did you hear from White-Lightning Joe yet?" She asked.

"I did." Seymour nodded.

"How was he?"

"Nora!" Georgina objected.

"I felt sorry for him. He needs a job."

"I hope you told your brother his history."

"Oh, he was upfront about that straight away." Seymour informed them, amused. "I've offered him part-time work to begin with, on a trial basis. He starts on Monday."

"You're so kind." Nora smiled.

Georgina sighed.

They reached the boxes. Humphrey, Nora, Cara, Seymour, Heather, Milton and Felix scrambled into box one. Georgina, Troy, Betty, Roger, Agnes and Cal entered box two. They could speak to each other by leaning over the polished balcony edge. Each box had a magnificent view.

Nora peeked across the auditorium to the Royal Box and was interested to see that the lights were on in there. With a small flutter of her tell-tale heart she wondered if the Duke of Cole would be in attendance. She thought it best not to ask Seymour and decided to just keep an eye out, but she chose a seat closest to the balcony, between Humphrey and Heather.

Danny arrived to take their drink orders. Cara pulled an enormous bag of maltesers from her bag and Milton shared around a bag of American marshmallows. They read the programmes, discussed the actors and admired the set which was simple, yet elegant and held an air of eeriness.

The lights began to dim.

"The Mayor has just arrived." Seymour pointed out, sipping his beer.

"And the chief of police." Cara said.

"Crumbs." Felix gawped.

Nora tried not to look at the Royal Box and focused on the stage, smiling at Humphrey who passed her a glass of wine.

As she took a sip, Heather nudged Nora's arm repetitively. When Nora looked at her, Heather gave a small head jerk across the auditorium. Nora swallowed her mouthful of wine hard, keeping a straight face when she saw the Duke of Cole enter the Royal Box with Jeeves and his butler, a red haired man who had worked at a large house outside Castletown and often popped into The Secondhand Bookworm.

The Duke of Cole glanced over at their box before settling down in his chair and accepting a programme from Jeeves. Nora observed all of this as she stared ahead, but watched on the periphery of her vision.

"The Duke of Cole is here!" Cara whispered.

"Don't point." Milton whispered back.

Felix sniggered into his coke.

"Oh yes." Nora said lightly.

Humphrey poured more wine into her glass.

Act One of The Woman in Black began. Arthur Kipp, portrayed by a famous English film and theatre actor walked onto stage, accompanied by an eager round of applause. Seymour grinned. The actor walked across the stage and picked up a manuscript of his story. Another actor entered and joined Arthur Kipps. The dialogue began.

Nora glanced over to the Royal Box. The Duke was watching the play, but he glanced over at her, met her gaze and held it. Nora smiled, looked away and leaned back, knowing now that she wouldn't get too terrified by The Woman in Black.

12 FELIX JOLLY, THE RADICAL

It was Halloween, but more importantly, it was *Slippery Saturday* in Castletown. The Halloween Silent Disco boat had moored on the river early that morning. Nora had gone for a jog at seven and met Harry along the road. Although she was suspicious that he had planned their meeting, she had found herself jogging with him down to the river where they had watched the large party boat arrive. Finally fed up with Harry imploring her to go to the disco with him, she had legged it back to her flat, showered, and pulled on her ghostly lady costume.

The ghostly lady costume was actually quite fantastic. It had a long grey skirt with tattered lace and ruffles. Then it had a black velvet bodice with black cobwebbing over it. Beneath that was a grey velvet chemise top that ended in vees at the wrist. There was a tiny black top hat that clipped to Nora's hair. It had a spidery black veil which was as though it wasn't even there. There was also a pair of black silk gloves.

Nora powdered her face with white make-up and swiped dark grey eye shadow around her eyes. Finally she finished with some black lipstick and thought she looked both wonderful and ghastly.

Castletown was busy when Nora walked down the hill. She had worried about feeling like a prize idiot in her costume, but it seemed as though everyone was in costume. A giraffe said good morning to her. Three zombies invited her to that afternoon's zombie walk. Glitter Angels with zombie faces were now advertising the silent disco boat. A group of escaped convicts were admiring the antique shop windows. Paul, who worked at the council and provided Christmas trees for the town, was putting up ragged black bunting and grey and orange balloons, while dressed as a zombiefied Willy Wonka, and there were stalls set up on the cobbles and along the streets, served by witches, mad clowns, devils, a hot dog, Dracula and Jigsaw from the Saw movies.

Nora read the flyer about the silent disco boat on the river as she approached The Secondhand Bookworm.

'Jump aboard the Dutch King, a three storey disco ship, for an evening of dancing and drinking with your undead friends in this Halloween silent disco party. From Halloween hits to hard-core disco tunes, pick the channel you want on your headphones. Come in fancy dress – the weirder and freakier the better! The Silent Disco boat opens at ten pm and sets sail up the river at eleven for all night partying.'

Nora folded the flyer and popped it into her bag. She then jumped as the perfect imitation of Heath Ledger's The Joker stepped up to her.

"Morning." Felix said.

"Oh my goodness!" Nora stared at her cousin.

The Joker grinned.

"I think we might win the Castletown Screamie Award tonight." Nora admired. "You look amazing."

"Thanks. 'Flattered emoji'." Felix appreciated.

"You're going to scare me all day though."

Felix sniggered.

Nora unlocked the shop, ran across the room and punched in the alarm code while Felix locked the door behind them.

"Wow! Scary times." Felix said, looking at the Halloween decorations.

"Shelob's Lair." Nora explained.

Felix looked alarmed.

"Today is Slippery Saturday." Nora said.

"I thought it was Halloween."

"Well, yes. But in the square there are some slimy critters. The town has declared it Slippery Saturday."

"Eeeeewwww." Felix gagged.

"I'm going to go and turn on the upstairs lights and prepare the children's room for my lunchtime reading session. Can you fill up the till?"

"Will do." Felix nodded and jumped in the swivel chair.

Nora sighed and set off, hoisting up her long tattered skirt as she mounted the stairs. In the children's room, Nora arranged the beanbags. Cara had put up cobwebs all over the ceiling and displayed some tombstones and plastic bones so it looked like a horrible room of horror, the perfect setting to read scary stories to innocent children.

In the attic room, Nora arranged some higgledy-piggledy books on the windowsill and glared down at the air conditioning unit belting out air from the estate agents next door. Nora frowned. It was chilly in the bookshop so it was ludicrous that the estate agents were using their air conditioning. She shook her head and set off back downstairs.

After putting the kettle on, examining the slime in the yard and turning on the little oil heater in the kitchen because it was so cold, Nora returned to the front where Felix was hoisting postcard spinners onto the street followed by sand pudding weights and then the black boxes of cheap paperbacks that clipped either side of the door.

A man wearing a t-shirt that had a pointing skeleton hand on it with the words 'I'm with creepy', was browsing a new copy of 'The Woman in Black'.

"Morning." He said, staring at Nora's costume.

"Morning." Nora smiled.

"Do you take national book tokens?"

"I'm afraid not."

"Forget it then." He said, turned and stormed off.

Nora stared after him.

"Excuse me!" Felix tutted. "That was very rude."

The man ignored him.

"Thanks, Felix." Nora appreciated, impressed with his morality.

"I'm standing up for principles from now on." Felix said importantly, stepping back inside the shop. "I'm fed up with being abused by customers."

Nora thought it was funny to see The Joker being high-minded.

"Watch it!" Felix then rebuked a large man dressed as Pinhead from Hellraiser.

Nora looked worried.

Pinhead ignored Felix, wandered off into the back of the shop and they heard him walking up the stairs.

"I'm going to mark the rest of these books up this morning." Nora said, dragging the last two boxes from her calls day behind the counter.

"Okay. Shall I check emails?"

"And 1517."

"Oh yeah." Felix pulled a face but it looked like he was continuously smiling with his Joker's mouth.

Nora snorted.

"Blasted Mrs Tentpole again." Felix moaned when he had listened to the answerphone messages.

Mrs Tentpole was a new regular who left endless messages moaning about them not being out of bed or awake and that they opened at nine so what did they think they were playing at not answering the phone.

"More Enid Blyton books?"

"Yes. Two. I'll go up and see if we have them."

"Okay." Nora smiled, sat down and grabbed a pencil. The pile of occult books for Spencer didn't fit under the counter with the reserved books, so Nora was piling them up under the stairs. She added two and hoped he would come in and buy loads that day.

A shadow loomed up to the opened doorway.

"Hiiiiiii. Great costume."

Nora saw Harry, holding a lead attached to Showgirl, the dog from the Greengrocer shop below his flat. Showgirl was large and smelly. She stood beside Harry as if contemplating peeing by the door.

"Oh. Hello again."

Harry had changed out of his jogging gear and now wore a black t-shirt with the image of chomping teeth on the front. It read 'Careful, I bite!' Harry saw Nora reading it so stuck out his chest.

"Can I bring Showgirl in?"

"No."

"Fair enough. I'm going to take her for a walk by the river. Do you want me to get two tickets for the Silent Disco boat?"

"Who for?"

"You and me."

"No."

"If you change your mind let me know. You've got my number."

Nora watched him wink at her, turn around and head off with Showgirl in tow. She gave an exasperated sigh.

"I'll be back." She heard him say.

Nora bit back a grin and typed *'TERMINATOR ALERT!!!'* on Skype chat and sent it to Seatown.

'Terminator? I swear we just had The Predator in here – Cal'

Nora giggled.

'I hope you and Roger are in costume – Nora' She sent.

'I'll send you a photo.' Cal replied.

A moment later Nora's iPhone screamed. She opened Cal's text and burst out laughing. A photograph of Roger dressed as Harry Potter stared back at her, looking disgruntled by the art books. Cal had taken it as a selfie, so Nora assumed that the hilarious blue Cookie Monster from Seseme Street was Cal.

'Awesome!' She texted back.

Felix returned empty handed so Nora showed him the photo from Seatown and he doubled up laughing. He then phoned Mrs Tentpole and quickly sobered when she told him what a waste of time it was phoning if they can't even bother to stock the right books.

"Old boot." Felix glowered, hanging up.

A customer arrived and asked to look at some Zombie books in the window so Felix headed over to show him as the telephone began to ring.

"Good morning, The Secondhand Bookworm."

"Morning, Nora." Georgina replied, sounding annoyed.

"Oh, hello. Everything alright?"

"No. I asked Felix to look up and price some books in Seatown yesterday and he hasn't marked them high enough."

"Oh dear." Nora grimaced.

"Hmm. I just told Roger off as well for putting the empty boxes in the kitchen instead of the van. Now I'm going to tell Felix off. Is he there?"

"He's with a customer at the moment."

"Tell him to phone me on my mobile. I'm at home."

"Okay. Will do." Nora replied.

"Thank you, Nora." Georgina sighed again and rang off.

Felix made a good sale, encouraging his customer to buy five books from the window. When the customer had paid and headed happily off, Nora gave him Georgina's message. His face fell.

"All Georgina does is tell me off lately." He whined.

"Well, she has been telling Roger off, too."

"She phoned me during Mass last Saturday evening. I had to slip out during the Gospel and answer it and it was to tell me off for not counting the float out properly."

"Oh dear."

"It must be the menopause." Felix decided and Nora laughed.

When he phoned Georgina back, Nora could hear Georgina moaning loudly at Felix. Felix pulled a face, apologising but when it went on and on, with Georgina becoming shrill, Felix burst into tears.

Nora stared.

Georgina fell silent.

"Ah-hoo-hoo-hoo, ah-hoo-hoo-hoo." Felix bawled. He glanced at Nora, trying not to laugh. Nora's eyes widened. "Sorry, Georgina. It won't happen again. Ah-hoo-hoo-hoo!"

Nora could hear Georgina speaking quietly now to Felix.

Felix nodded, sniffing loudly and trying not to laugh.

"Okay, Georgina. Yes. Sorry, again. Thank you. Bye." He said and hung up.

"I can't believe you did that!" Nora exclaimed.

"Well, she obviously wanted to make me cry." Felix shrugged.

"Felix Jolly. *The Radical*."

"What?" Felix asked.

"You're like Felix Holt, the Radical." Nora was impressed.

"Felix who?" Felix grinned.

"Felix Holt, the Radical! It's a George Elliot novel. Don't go starting any riots now." Nora said. "Or manslaughter any unsuspecting constables.

"Ooo-eeer." Felix said and then laughed.

Nora spent the morning marking up the rest of the books while Felix dealt with customers of various appearances. They had a trade sale of over three hundred pounds, sold a set of Folio society books, numerous Shire Guides, new Ordinance Survey maps, armfuls of new Wordsworth novels, lots of occult books, children's books and twelve Penguin book mugs. They were worn out by noon.

"Excuse me. Where is the children's room for the spooky readings?" A lady with two boys asked.

"Up the stairs and round into the back." Nora replied, preparing he little pile of Edward Gorey books.

"Thanks. Is it starting soon?"

"In about five minutes." Nora smiled.

Felix smirked.

"Oh, I wish I could hear it. You should read them down here."

"No, there's too much people traffic." Nora said.

Harry returned.

"Hiiiiii. I'm here with my nephew for the spooky readings." He announced, dragging a teenage boy in by the arm.

"Oh." Nora stared.

"Upstairs, isn't it?" He asked.

"Hmm." Nora gave Felix a look.

Felix snorted and sniggered into a book.

"Great." Nora muttered once Harry and his protesting nephew had gone upstairs. "I bet Cara told him I was doing the reading."

"Probably." Felix sniggered. "I'll run up and snap a few photos at some point. When it falls quiet for a bit down here."

"Okay, but don't leave the till unattended for too long. Are you hungry?"

"I can eat these crisps until you've finished." Felix replied.

"Okay. Well, it sounds like there are so many people the floor might collapse. I hope they've saved me a beanbag."

Felix sniggered again so Nora left him, heading upstairs with her copies of 'The Gashlycrumb Tinnies' and Oscar Wilde's 'The Canterville Ghost', the last one because she wanted to be a bit classy, plus she had loved the movie with Patrick Stewart when she was a child.

The children's room was packed with children and parents and they clapped when Nora arrived. She blushed but then bowed and approached a large blue beanbag by the A-K bookcase. Nora recognised a reporter from the Castletown magazine, so she arranged her costume carefully, sat up straight and smiled at the children.

"Happy Halloween!" She said.

"Happy Halloween." Everyone chorused.

One child burst into tears so was carried hastily away.

"I am the Ghostly Lady of The Secondhand Bookworm!" Nora then said in a ghostly voice.

"Ooooo." The parents replied.

Harry was grinning at her stupidly, gripping his nephew's arm to stop him running away.

"And I like to read from all the books in this shop. Do you like to read?"

"Yeeeeees!" The children nodded.

202

"And would you like me to read you a story?"

"Yeeeeeeees!" The children screamed, making Nora flinch.

"Today I am going to tell you about some very naughty children, and what happened to them when they didn't listen to their mummies and daddies. The children are known as The Gashlycrumb Tinnies."

Several giggles.

Nora cleared her throat.

"I shall begin." She opened the first page and stared. "Ahem. Right. A is for Amy who fell down the stairs."

She showed the picture around of a girl in a white dress, falling down some steps.

"B is for Basil assaulted by Bears."

There were gasps and 'ooooos'. Harry took Nora's photo.

"C is for Clara who wasted away." She showed them a picture of a sickly, thin girl laying in a large bed.

The children laughed when she got to 'F is for Fanny sucked dry by a leech' and 'L is for Leo who swallowed some tacks'. They all clapped when she had finished and then she started to read 'The Canterville Ghost'.

"*When Mr Hiram B. Otis , the American Minister, bought Canterville Chase, everyone told him he was doing a very foolish thing,*" Nora began and sat back happily as all eyes were upon her and she told the story.

Midway through, Felix ran loudly up the stairs and distracted everyone by taking some photos and then tearing back down again; one child threw up some Halloween sweets and several left to use the public toilets. When Nora finished exactly at one o'clock, she received a round of applause and posed for photographs with the books and several children.

"That was fun!" Nora told Felix when she was back down.

"I'm starving." Felix replied.

"I'll just make a cup of tea because I'm dying of thirst and then you can go off for lunch."

"Okay." Felix agreed.

Nora met Harry and his nephew by the stairwell.

"Did you enjoy the story?" She asked them both.

"Yes!" Harry said enthusiastically.

"It was alright. He fancies you." Harry's nephew said.

Harry just grinned.

"You don't say." Nora muttered, bade them goodbye and hid in the kitchen to make tea.

When she finally emerged, Felix grabbed his wallet and set off to buy some lunch, leaving Nora texting Georgina to tell her the spooky story time was a great success!

13 GERTRUDE JEKYL AND MR HYDE

The Gorey-ent Express chugged into town earlier that day, but couldn't turn around because of the fayre on the cobbles in the square. Nora and Felix watched as stalls were moved aside and people shook their fists or took photos while getting covered in green smoke. They were giggling at the zombies and witches jumping from the carriages and falling into the stalls when a scream told Nora she had received a text message.

"Let me know what happens." Nora said and returned behind the counter to sit down. "I'll go for my lunch when the train has finally gone."

"It's turned a bit further. Ooops, it almost knocked over the war memorial." Felix commentated.

Nora chuckled and opened her text.

'Just picked up a copy of 'The Woman in Black' movie in Piertown. Fancy watching it tonight? xxx' Humphrey had written.

Nora smiled.

'Sounds fun. My place? Xxx' Nora replied.

'I'll bring a take-away. See you later xxxx' Humphrey affirmed.

Nora placed her phone back under the counter, noticing two men walking past the window, watching the Gorey-ent express. She straightened up.

"Afternoon." Spencer greeted, stepping down into The Secondhand Bookworm. "This is Mal."

Nora peered curiously at Spencer's friend. Like Spencer, Mal fancied himself as an amateur exorcist, clairvoyant and medium. Both of them believed in fairies.

"Hello, Nora." Mal smiled.

Nora jumped.

Mal had very hazel eyes which were almost red, a tiny thin moustache and a goatee beard. He looked like the devil.

"Hello." She said warily.

"Anything for me?" Spencer asked.

"Well. As a matter of fact." Nora turned around and began to load up the counter with piles of occult books.

"Wow!" Spencer gasped, ecstatic.

He and Mal pored over them, speaking excitedly. Nora pushed the books over to the side so they moved out of the way as a customer approached.

"Hello." The man said quietly.

"Hello." Nora replied with a friendly smile.

Felix was sniggering to himself, pointing and then clutching his sides. Nora assumed more mayhem was occurring with the Gorey-ent Express.

"My name is Mr Hyde. Are these pages coated?" The man asked.

Nora stared at him uncertainly.

"Coated?"

"Yes. I work in a laboratory so I know all about chemicals and paper diseases." Mr Hyde said.

"Oh. Paper diseases?"

"For instance, a live flu virus can live on paper money for seventeen days." Mr Hyde revealed.

Nora's face fell.

"Really?"

"Yes, germs survive on paper for over seventy two hours. I detected herpes and cocaine on a copy of 'Fifty Shades of Grey'."

Nora decided not to believe Mr Hyde. She wondered if he was really Doctor Jekyll, turned into Mr Hyde.

"Oh dear. Well, these books have all been fumigated before being placed on our shelves." Nora said, aware of Spencer and Mal glancing at her, smirking.

"Do you stock Persephone Books?" A woman asked, hoisting herself down the step and approaching the counter.

"Erm..." Nora looked at Felix who drew his attention away from the window to deal with the lady.

"I am glad to hear about the fumigation." Mr Hyde said. "I'll take these then, please."

"Thank you. Would you like a bag?"

Mr Hyde pondered the area where the bags were kept.

"How about a cotton bag?"

"They're two pounds each." Nora said.

"I'll take one." Mr Hyde nodded, took out his wallet and paid with a twenty pound note.

Nora took it warily, gave him his change, put the books in his cotton bag and said goodbye. She then slipped the twenty pound note under the till tray for safe keeping.

"I'll definitely have these!" Spencer said, pushing a large pile towards Nora. "Where did you get them?"

"A man's collection at his house along Park Town Road." Nora explained.

"They're brilliant. Can you keep these aside for me so I can check. They change the covers so I forget which ones I have."

"Sure." Nora smiled.

"We're going upstairs to have a look in the occult section. By the way, love the costume."

Nora had actually forgotten she was wearing one. She glanced down.

"Oh yes. Thanks."

The Gorey-ent Express chugged past, making Nora and Felix and the lady he was serving cough as green billowing smoke puffed into the room. Once the air had cleared and Spencer and Mal had gone upstairs, Nora announced she was going to go and get some lunch.

The Slippery Saturday Fayre offered lots of disgusting things to look at and buy. Nora met Crossword Lady who asked her a literary clue for that day's crossword which Nora answered while distracted by a tank of enormous centipedes. She was helping on the Slimy Critters stall which was surrounded by children.

When she saw a tarantula, Nora hastily ran away.

A bowl of bobbing apples with plastic spiders was drawing a crowd. There was a large spinning machine that offered a prize or a spell if it stopped on a specific picture. Nora had a go and almost got cursed. Fortunately she won a chocolate frog instead.

The Harry Potter stalls had sweets, wands, books, stuffed toys of owls, cats, toads and bats, cauldrons and ornaments. Another stall was serving food from a spooky menu. Nora felt sick at the offer of witches (fish) fingers and Blood (beef) Burgers. In the end she bought a chicken salad sandwich from the delicatessen and headed back to The Secondhand Bookworm.

After lunch, a man telephoned to ask if he could bring some books along for sale. Nora agreed and met him at his car which he parked on double yellow lines outside the Indian Restaurant round the corner. He had a boot filled with gardening books in lovely condition so Nora offered him fifty pounds for the lot. They then carried them into The Secondhand Bookworm, placed them all behind the counter, Nora paid him and she and Felix set to work marking them up.

"These are lovely books about Gertrude Jekyll." Nora praised, thumbing through a particularly nice hardback.

"Oh, I've seen her books before." Felix said.

"Yes. She was a British horticulturist. She created about four hundred gardens all over Britain, Europe and the United States. Beautiful designs."

"Oh. Are they Gertrude Jekyll books?" A woman asked.

She had been browsing upstairs and had an armful of craft books.

"Yes. They've just come in."

"May I have a look?"

"May I have a look too?"

"I'd like to see them as well."

Nora and Felix stared as another lady and a man dressed as a zombie surrounded them.

"Go ahead!" Nora said hastily and handed them out.

"It's warm in here!" A woman in a vampire costume exclaimed.

"Oh. I thought it was a bit chilly." Nora admitted, giving Felix a look.

"No. It's very warm."

"Can you check your computer and see if you have a certain book in stock?" The vampire asked.

"Sorry, we don't list our books on the computer."

The vampire sighed and her fangs dropped out. Nora watched in disgust as she bent down, picked them up off the carpet and popped them back in without even wiping them. Felix might have been grimacing but his Joker make-up gave the continuous impression he was smiling.

"Then do you know if you have a certain book?" She asked.

"What are you after?" Nora inquired.

"The Moonstone by Wilkie Collins."

"Oh, we probably have a copy or two." Nora said and Felix jumped up to show the lady where to look.

The three Gertrude Jekyll fans bickered among themselves and ended up buying several books each. Nora got the fifty pounds she had paid out back in no time so the rest of the gardening books that she and Felix priced were pure profit.

Tobey, who worked in the bank and sometimes met Nora for lunch in the secret garden down River Road, walked past dressed as a vampire and waved. Several children with their faces painted ran in and screamed and shouted around the shop for half an hour. Lots of people commented favourably on the decorations and their costumes and a travelling salesman sold them some ceramic pumpkins which Nora displayed along the till. Spencer and Mal returned and spent two hundred pounds between them. Mal invited Nora and Felix on a Fairy Hunt the next day but they politely declined.

Soon, the zombies began to gather for the afternoon Zombie Walk. The fayre began to pack away with loud bangs and crashes as stalls were dismounted. Fortunately it had all cleared out when the Gorey-ent Express arrived again to deposit more costume wearers from the train station. This time the large Halloween Train turned easily into the square and set off back to the station happily.

Felix was reading a Shire Library book from the spinner on the counter, about 'The Victorian Criminal' while Nora sat thinking.

"I'm going to start a Book Club." She then announced.

Felix looked up.

"Really?"

"Yes. But not your usual Book Club. My Book Club is going to be very special because I have a series of rare and unknown detective mystery novels, six in total, and I think it would be fun to have a Book Club read and talk about those together. Georgina said I could host it here. So shove over. I'm going to make a poster and stick it in the window."

Felix got up and moved onto the wooden stool.

"Can I come?"

"If you like." Nora smiled.

"When are you going to start it?"

"Probably over Christmas and the New Year. It will only be about six or seven weeks."

"Not next month?"

"No. Georgina mentioned doing a run up to Black Friday this year so I think November will be put aside for that. Plus, I want to read them myself first so I get familiar with the stories. Then I can lead the club better."

Several customers entered the shop so Nora left Felix to deal with them while she designed her poster, listening with half an ear and a baffled smirk as her cousin dealt with zombies, witches, aliens and Hansel and Gretel.

"Do you know where the Zombie Apocalypse parties are being held?"

"Are you a bookshop?"

"I've lost my false teeth. Have you seen them?"

"Are you Dave Bone?"

"Where is the refugee camp?"

Nora was distracted by the last question and amused by Felix's answers and expressions, even as The Joker.

A man dressed as Batman entered the shop.

"My nemesis is here!" He exclaimed, staring at Felix.

"Oh. Hahahaha." Felix laughed. *"Inside. He's laughing red and black and red and black till there's*

nothing left to laugh. Until, almost tenderly, he turns
inside out through his mouth."

Batman and Nora stared at Felix.

"It's a quote from Heath Ledger's Joker diary." Felix said.

"You really researched your character." Batman was impressed. "You wanted me! Here I am!" He then said in a low, gravely, Batman movie voice.

Nora rolled her eyes and left them to their recreation of a scene where Batman interrogates The Joker in 'The Dark Night' movie. Several customers watched and clapped when they had finished. Batman went off to browse, leaving Felix serving a Hobbit.

When Nora's Book Club poster was complete, she printed it out and held it up. It read:

NEW BOOK CLUB

A six week book club to begin at The Secondhand Bookworm in December

Would you like to join a book club to read the novels of a forgotten author?

Books provided

Father Ulysses E. Flood was the parish priest of Saint Aldhelm's outside of Castletown in the 1930's and wrote six detective novels based loosely on his years as a Catholic priest and amateur sleuth

More information inside!

Places limited

Speak to Nora Jolly

"That sounds great!" Felix said after he had read it.

"Thanks. Hopefully it'll get some interest. I've also made a chart for names. I think eight people will be enough. If more are interested, I can always run another one once it's finished."

"It sounds fun. Sign me up!"

"Great! My first member." Nora took the chart from the printer and passed it to Felix. "It will be one day a week, after work, here. So you have to commit."

"I will!" Felix promised, writing his name and phone number down.

Nora pinned it next to White-Lightning Joe's forensic sketch with a pleased smile. She then stuck the poster up in the window. Then she decided on a plan to fast-read all the Father Ulysses E. Flood mystery novels. She was looking forward to it.

Nora and Felix sat chatting about the Book Club while numerous customers came and went.

Billy, who ran the antique centre and Passageway Antiques with another local man named Mr Sykes, popped in and said he had discovered a box of leather books he'd like to sell. They were just sitting on his shelf doing nothing. Felix told him to bring them down and they'd have a look, so Billy said he would do that next week.

"Last of the big spenders." A lady waving postcards joked.

"How much for cash?" A man asked Felix.

"Three floors of books! I may be some time." Someone dressed as Gandalf said.

"Do you have 'The Arsenal Stadium Mystery' by Leonard Gribble?" An old man demanded.

"Is the cemetery near here?" Three hags asked.

"Have you got a bus time table?" A lady with a turban enquired.

"Was this town ever invaded?" A very skinny man wanted to know.

By the time the zombies had gathered, Nora and Felix were exhausted.

Nora's mobile rang and she saw it was Georgina. She showed Felix the caller ID so he pretended to cry. Nora's eyes widened so he doubled over sniggering and laughing.

"Hello, Georgina."

"Hi, Nora. I'm in Piertown and have noticed signs and posters going up about Black Friday at the end of November."

Nora mouth 'Black Friday' to Felix, who was impressed at her premonition.

"I think it would be a good idea if we start putting books aside that they can sell off cheap. We don't want to do a general discount because we have a good selection of rare and antiquarian books, but I think we could maybe have a sale section or something? It would be good to start advertising it now, so can you design posters for Castletown and Seatown, please?"

"Sure. Oh, I just put up a poster for my Book Club. Is that alright?"

Georgina laughed.

"That's fine. But maybe put it aside, on the wall, until Black Friday is over."

"Okay." Nora nodded. "Do you think Black Friday will work in Castletown?"

"Well, we can give it a go." Georgina said.

They rang off and Nora relayed to Felix Georgina's plans. Nora then set about designing a Black Friday poster. She googled to see when it would take place and read up that some retailers Black Friday sales began on Wednesday and carried through to Saturday. That year, Black Friday took place after Thanksgiving in the USA and retailers reveal massive discounts on their wares for the Christmas period.

A scream announced a text message for Nora. She saw it was from Cara.

'Seymour has just announced to his troupe that they will be performing 'Little Shop of Horrors' next Halloween!!'

Nora's eyes lit up.

'That's fantastic. I'm always singing 'Suddenly Seymour' to him xxx'

'He told me! LOL. I've changed his ringtone to that. More news later! P.S. Are you going to go to the Halloween Silent Disco Boat?'

'I wasn't planning to. Are you?'

'I thought it would be fun. We could meet on board at 10pm?'

'I'll ask Humphrey. He's bringing a scary movie over tonight. Wanna join us?'

'That'd be awesome. Then we can walk down to the Disco! I'll tell Seymour.'

'Be at mine for seven xxx'

'I'll bring popcorn and we'll dress up xxx'

'And you can help me carve my pumpkin xxx' Nora smirked and texted Humphrey.

'Mind if Cara and Seymour come for movie night? How do you fancy taking a voyage on the Haunted Disco Ship afterwards? xx' She sent, and went back to her poster.

A moment later, Humphrey replied.

'Sounds great! Shall I dress up? Xxx'

'It's a must! Xxx'

'I can get to yours for six xx'

'See you then xxx' Nora sent and smiled.

A man dressed as Riff Raff from The Rocky Horror Picture Show entered The Secondhand Bookworm.

"Do you have a copy of 'Night Terrors – the ghost stories of E F Benson'?" He asked a staring Felix.

"Oh. Erm…it's possible there could be a copy in the window." He replied.

Felix rummaged with Riff Raff and found him a paperback. Riff Raff was delighted.

"With a bit of a mind flip, you can achieve anything." He said and left, carrying his book.

"I'm looking for Gaston Leroux's 'The Mystery of the Yellow Room'." A purple witch said.

With her was another woman, dressed as Bavmorda from the movie 'Willow'. She had a very spikey crown and looked quite scary.

"Oh. I can check for you." Felix replied.

"We have that in the window, too." Nora said and pointed. "There."

"Don't point at me!" Bavmorda exclaimed dramatically. She then pretended to call down bolts of lightning. Nora laughed.

Buffy the Vampire Slayer arrived.

"Hi! Any books about lace making?"

Nora pointed her upstairs.

"How long has this shop been here?! I've never noticed it before!" A man exclaimed.

"Oh. For some time." Nora assured.

"Does the Bishop live in Castletown?" An old lady enquired.

"No." Nora replied.

"Oh. But the Duke does."

"Er…yes."

"Can you give him this invitation? It's to my son's wedding."

"Erm…sure." Nora smiled awkwardly and accepted a cream envelope. She then grinned to herself.

The zombie walk began just as Nora printed out her Black Friday Poster. She showed Felix who read it aloud. It read:

BLACK FRIDAY at The Secondhand Bookworm!
The day of BARGAINS is almost upon us
From November 19th – November 24th we will be celebrating the lead up to Black Friday with discounts and bargains on selected BOOKS and book related items
Don't miss out!

Save the date!
COMING SOON to Castletown!
Happy Thanksgiving.

Felix sniggered.

"That should do it." Nora said and walked over to the door. She closed it slightly to remove her Book Club poster. She then tacked up the Black Friday poster and placed her poster on the wall behind the door. "I'll make some Book Club flyers. Then locals can take them." She decided.

Felix watched the Zombie Walk while Nora worked on her flyers.

Groans, screams and moaning filled the air outside. Staggering, lurching zombies surged down the hill accompanied to the sounds of cap guns firing. Michael Jackson's 'Thriller' then blared out and zombies and visitors alike began to sing and dance. Nora ignored them, noticing Felix dancing out of the corner of her eye.

When the zombie walk had finished there was a round of applause.

"The Mayor and the town council planners and members are gathering on the cobbles." Felix said.

"Oh. They're probably going to announce the winner of The Castletown Screamie Award." Nora realised.

She jumped up and joined Felix in the doorway, almost tripping over her long tattered skirt.

"Oh, and there's the Duke of Cole." Felix added.

Nora caught her breath and spotted him, tall and handsome in the crowd, accompanied by Jeeves.

The Mayor of Castletown gave a speech through a megaphone, congratulating the town on a successful Shriek-Week and thanking the Duke for accepting his invitation to join them for the end of the Halloween festival. The Duke smiled and shook the Mayor's hand. The Mayor then announced the winner of The

Castletown Screamie Award. All the town's retailers and shop owners were either waiting in their doorways or in the street.

"And the winner of this year's Castletown Screamie award is…THE SECONDHAND BOOKWORM!'

Nora and Felix jumped, stared and then blinked. Everyone turned to look at them and clapping erupted.

"Oh my goodness!" Nora whispered.

"What do we do?" Felix asked.

"Well, one of us will have to go and collect it!"

"You go!"

"No, you go!"

"No, you run the shop!" Felix whispered hard.

Sam from the butcher's wolf whistled and called out Nora's name. Blushing beneath her make-up, Nora left the safety of the doorway and began across the road, walking among the people (mainly zombies) and grinning with embarrassment.

"Grrr." A Werewolf said.

"Argh!" A zombie congratulated.

"Well done!" Alice and Philip from the delicatessen called.

Sam and his brother Tim were chanting Nora's name.

Nora found herself walking towards the Duke, who held the award, smiling at her.

"Congratulations." The Duke of Cole said and leaned closer to her as he handed her the award. "When I learned The Secondhand Bookworm had won, I accepted the Mayor's invitation to come down and present the award."

"Among the zombies, Your Grace? For me?" Nora whispered back.

He laughed and shook her hand.

"Thank you, Your Grace." Nora accepted, held up the award and everyone clapped.

"The Secondhand Bookworm is our only bookshop in Castletown and I would recommend paying it a visit." The Mayor shouted into his megaphone, making everyone wince.

"Thank you." Nora appreciated.

"Speech! Speech!" Sam hollered and winked when Nora gave him a warning look.

Fortunately the Mayor moved onto other announcement about the ongoing entertainment including the Halloween trail, with chocolate prizes, the Halloween Silent Disco Boat, the zombie parties, a Ghosts of Castletown readings and lecture in the town hall. Nora savoured standing next to the Duke who didn't seem to be listening to the Mayor.

"Seeing as I'm here, I'll show my patronage to the winner of 'The Castletown Screamie Award' and pay The Secondhand Bookworm a visit." He told her.

"Thank you, Your Grace." Nora smiled.

"Wonderful costume by the way." He murmured and Nora blushed.

The crowd began to disperse and many people headed towards The Secondhand Bookworm. Shop owners and locals congratulated Nora as she walked with the Duke, tailed by Jeeves. The Mayor and several council members followed eagerly. Nora spent the short trip thanking everyone and when she was finally through the doorway she placed the award in the window by the pumpkin candles.

Nora left the Duke to browse under the stares of the many people filling the shop and accompanied by Jeeves, the Mayor and other important people. Felix looked harassed but pleased as he ran endless sales through the till. Nora joined him and bagged up books, thanked people for the congratulations and smiled at the comments of praise about the decorations. When she had a moment free, Nora sent a text message to Cara and

Georgina to let them know about the award, and also
Skyped Seatown. Cara phoned, squealing with delight.
Roger and Cal expressed their jealousy. Georgina sent
through *'well done!'*

The Duke of Cole purchased a mountaineering book
while the Mayor loudly praised the decorations.

"May I take one of these?" The Duke asked, picking
up Nora's Book Club flyer.

"Oh. Yes. Please do." She nodded.

He read it, smiled and placed it inside his book,
giving Nora a knowing look.

"Congratulations once again, Miss Jolly." The Duke
said, nodding at Felix as well.

"Thank you, Your Grace." Nora beamed.

"Thank you, sir, Your Grace, sir." Felix stared.

The Duke tapped his book with the Book Club flyer
in, bid them goodbye and set off with Jeeves who smiled
at Nora thoughtfully.

When the madness had finished, Felix and Nora
accepted a complimentary round of pumpkin juice from
the delicatessen and flopped into their seats. It was
almost closing time.

"I can't believe we won!" Nora said, taking a grateful
sip.

"I know! 'Shocked emoji'." Felix nodded.

"What a Happy Halloween." Nora bade him.

"Do you think the Duke of Cole would actually come
to your Book Club?" Felix asked.

"Who knows?" Nora shrugged, but hid her smile
behind her glass.

Felix looked at her suspiciously.

They began to bring the postcard spinners in from
outside as a few lingering zombies browsed through the
art books in the front of the shop. While Felix hoisted in
the black boxes of cheap paperback, Nora shooed out
Doctor Who, Professor McGonagall and Chucky, turned

off the upstairs lights, locked up the kitchen and served the last remaining zombies.

"Wow. What a great day. Over a thousand pounds!" Nora said as Felix locked the door.

"Bonus time!" He celebrated. "I'm not looking forward to Black Friday. Won't it halve our takings?"

"It's difficult to say. It could level out with extra buyers, or double the takings with extra, extra buyers. I think Georgina might be planning discounting all our tat. People love to think they get a bargain." Nora mused.

Felix sniggered, conspiratorially.

The cashed up, bade goodbye to Roger and Cal (who were sulking), turned off the lights, set the alarm and scrambled out of The Secondhand Bookworm. Nora locked up and gazed fondly at the Castletown Screamie Award in the window.

"Well done." A man dressed as a zombified Santa Clause said, stopping next to them.

"Thanks." Nora smiled.

"Oh. You're having a Black Friday event. I'll make sure I come along." He said, reading Nora's poster.

Nora and Felix looked at one another. Felix stuck up his thumbs.

"Happy Halloween, Felix." Nora said.

"Happy Halloween, Nora." Felix returned.

They bade goodbye and Nora set off up the hill, looking forward to 'The Woman in Black' movie, a cruise on the haunted Silent Disco Ship, and already planning what would probably be an interesting and eventful Black Friday at The Secondhand Bookworm!

THE END

ALSO IN THE SERIES

'The Secondhand Bookworm'
'Nora and The Secondhand Bookworm'
'Christmas at The Secondhand Bookworm'
'Summer at The Secondhand Bookworm'
'Black Friday at The Secondhand Bookworm'
'Book Club at The Secondhand Bookworm'

Available in paperback and Kindle

Watch for more novels in the Bookworm series

Also by the author

'House of Villains'
Available now from Amazon

ABOUT THE AUTHOR

Emily Jane Bevans lives on the south coast of England. For ten years she worked in, and helped to manage, a family chain of antiquarian bookshops in Sussex. She is the co-founder and co-director of a UK based Catholic film production apostolate 'Mary's Dowry Productions'. She writes, edits, produces, directs, narrates and sometimes acts for the company's numerous historical and religious films on the lives of the Saints and English Martyrs. She also likes to write contemporary and historical fiction.

MARY'S DOWRY PRODUCTIONS

Mary's Dowry Productions is a Catholic Film
Production Apostolate founded in 2007 to bring the lives
of the Saints and English Martyrs, English Catholic
heritage and history to film and DVD. Mary's Dowry
Productions' unique film production style has been
internationally praised for not only presenting facts,
biographical information and historical details but a
prayerful and spiritual film experience. Many of the
films of Mary's Dowry Productions have been broadcast
on EWTN, BBC and SKY.
For a full listing of films and more information visit:

www.marysdowryproductions.org

EMILY JANE BEVANS

Made in United States
Orlando, FL
13 August 2023

36047110R00146